HiS LONELY ROAR

ALEKSEY OLKHOVENKO

World Castle Publishing, LLC
Pensacola, Florida
Copyright © 2024 Aleksey Olkhovenko
Paperback ISBN: 9798891261860
eBook ISBN: 9798891261877
First Edition World Castle Publishing, LLC, May 6, 2024
http://www.worldcastlepublishing.com

Licensing Notes

Cover: Cover Designs by Karen
Cover-designs-by-karen.com
Editor: Karen Fuller

To Mr. Holmes, whose unfaltering perspicuity inspired a world of imagination.

CHAPTER 1

The train of time forever carries sins and blunders. Its engine bellows like a coal-powered monster, its huffing and puffing never reaching an end. The wheels never stop spinning. Forever going around and around, they caress the tracks with the force of a blacksmith's hammer on perfect metal, a strike that's graceful yet will forge a sword worth crying over. The train of time moves with uniformity, as constant as gravity's eternal reign. The headlights blind, and the whistle roars.

The train of time's conductor is unknown. The destination—unknown. The reason for its existence—unknown. All that is known about the train of time is that it exists, it moves, and its timetable is without flaw — when it arrives at your station, it is time to face your past, your sins, and your blunders.

A train whooshed into the station, reeling as it braked to a stop. To Hans, there was nothing out of the ordinary about this train. He had seen trains every day for almost five years now. The doors opened, the conductor announcing that they would be taking a short break before departing for the next station, a town that Hans would probably never be able to explore. But assumptions are often dangerous. After all, the train of time had reached its destination.

As his eyes wandered around his little station operating cabin, Hans observed the trinkets he had accumulated on his shelves during his time as the stationmaster of the Brumont train station. He noticed his unopened candle, a gift from his mother from when he was younger. He loved burning candles at home, but this one was too special for him to burn. His eyes glanced at his favorite bonsai tree, which he had raised and trimmed with extreme care. There was nothing as therapeutic as trimming bonsai trees.

Of course, Hans' gaze couldn't avoid the massive timetable that hung above his window, which allowed him to keep track of the carefully calculated maneuvers of the trains entering his platform. When he first started, he'd use this table to inform weary travelers when their train would arrive. He'd worked long enough now not to need it.

But what always caught Hans' eye was his most prized possession, given to him by his grandfather. And it was what the ominous men wearing black suits requested when they came up to the window.

The train that had pulled into the platform was completely normal. And Hans had dealt with various types of train riders before. But this was something he had never experienced in the past. He didn't have time to examine his favorite trinket because three men in sharp, suave formal wear approached him.

They each wore three-piece suits, well-polished dress shoes, and heavily-darkened sunglasses. Their pitch-black hair was slicked back, completing the classy look. The man leading this refined charge spoke before Hans could welcome them to Brumont.

"I'll put it simply. I won't waste your time. We came here for the flowers," the man said in a loud, demanding voice. People had asked Hans in the past about Brumont's flower shop. It was well known for its bountiful bouquets of fresh, lovely-smelling flowers and gorgeous paintings hanging from its walls.

Though intimidated by the man, Hans responded, "I'm pleased to help you, sir. The flower shop is right down the road. Head about five blocks down, and you should see it. Please tell Jasmine I said hello. Welcome to Brumont!" Hans tried to speak to these men the same way he would to any customer. But this time, choking through his usual, cheerful greeting took some effort.

"You misunderstand, sir. I want *your* flowers."

"I think I do misunderstand. I don't sell any flowers."

"We know that you have them," the man insisted. "I assure you that we will ransack this place until we find the flowers that you possess. We always finish our job, sir."

And that's when it hit Hans. Looking back at the decoration that he was trying to admire earlier, he became worried. He had always believed that it was just a decoration. Now, he wasn't so sure.

"What have you done, grandpa?" Hans had thought nothing of the flowers the men seemed to be after. They were three beautiful heathers his grandfather said he had collected himself. Their dazzling white petals amazed Hans every time he caught a glimpse of them. And catching a whiff of the

flower would make a heavenly sensation descend upon anyone's nose. At first, he was confused as to why his grandfather had given them to him.

When he first received them, he remembered thinking, *"Why didn't he just go to Jasmine's flower shop? Why go through all the effort?"*

Hans quickly learned why. After a couple of days of surviving under *his* care, Hans thought that the flowers were resilient. After a couple of weeks, he began to consider them creepy. And after a couple of months, he had to admit they were *magic*.

The head honcho of the men in black followed Hans' eyes to the heathers, sitting peacefully in their porcelain pot. Not distracted by the other trinkets, he pointed out, "It seems you have what we're looking for. Hand them over."

"Why?" Hans questioned immediately. Though the flowers did seem to be special, he couldn't understand why the men would take a train all the way to

Brumont to retrieve them. After all, this was Hans' precious belonging. He considered the blessing of the heathers staying alive for months on end a lucky charm. There was no reason for him to hand them over to these crooks.

"We don't want to cause you any trouble. I warned you already what the consequences would be if you tried to block us from completing our job," the mysterious man reminded Hans.

Another of the men firmly demanded, "Hand it over. We will not ask again."

"No," Hans said very simply. As soon as the word left his lips, he realized that he had made the wrong decision. The two men lurking in the back of the civilized formation stepped forward. As one of them reached into the window, too fast for Hans to stop, the other jammed his palm right at Hans' chin, cleanly knocking him out.

As he floated out of consciousness, Hans saw the first man secure the heathers into a bag the men had brought with them.

The man who had knocked Hans out forced open the door to his minuscule stationmaster cabin, picked him up, and walked back out like a hunter lugging a prized bounty from a successful hunt.

The men were swift in completing their mission. Just as quickly as they had obtained their objective, they seamlessly stepped onto the motionless train. Had Hans been in his cabin, a look at his timetable would have informed him the train was ready to depart. This time, he got to experience it live. After all the men entered, the train doors closed, and the train of time was yet again on its way.

CHAPTER 2

When Hans awoke from his unconscious slumber, his eyes were struck with an uncomfortable amount of color. Back in Brumont, the town he had been born and raised in, the train station was rather dull. All he could see for miles, sitting in his little booth, were rolling hills and occasional cars driving on the highway, which snaked across the landscape—a strand of spaghetti alongside the railroad tracks. Though it was barren, it was comforting for Hans. He had become used to the dullness of life.

His surroundings were now anything but dull. He tried to examine them while remaining as motionless as possible. He knew that he was still under the control of his captors. They were marching with discipline and no emotion, walking in the same formation they had appeared in front of Hans. Just as he was used to Brumont, these men seemed to be used to this jarring world. Hans was at the back of the formation, with one of the men clutching his shoulders tightly and the other his calves.

Thankfully, the men couldn't see his eyes. This gave him the perfect opportunity to look around. Not only was he struck by the astoundingly bright purples, oranges, and various shades of blue that surrounded him, but also the flora and fauna that the colors belonged to.

The men were walking high above the canopy, with colorful leaves making up the visible landscape. It seemed they were walking on a mountain that jutted out from the rather-flat terrain. Hans could see the rough edges of the side of the mountain, where shrubs were populated with glimmering sky-blue creatures that looked like mice with comically large ears, eyes almost as large as their ears, and noses that quivered slightly. As the men approached them, the rodents scampered away.

From the forest, Hans could see a sky-blue glimmer shine through the canopy, just like the rodents but with much greater brightness. He imagined it was another creature–perhaps a deer or a bear.

The men walked across a thick log suspended in the air across a ravine. Any misstep would mean falling into the chasm to which there seemed to be no bottom. Leaves with patterns Hans had never seen before hung off the earthy brown log. Though they resembled the heart-shaped leaves he had often noticed on Brumont's trees, there was something uncanny about them.

Of course, these leaves would do nothing to catch the men if they were to fall off the log. The height didn't seem to bother them, though. They walked masterfully across without any hesitation in their steps.

As soon as they reached the other side

of the log, the men dropped Hans on the ground and walked inside of a tree trunk. *"We're here," he* realized. He did not know where "here" was. He only knew that he had a moment to be alone.

Hans realized that both his hands and ankles were tied. He did not feel anything physical around them. Instead, it felt like an invisible force which stopped them from moving. A force he couldn't overcome. Hans lay motionless on the ground, his hope of escaping waning.

He didn't think he would ever experience feeling trapped again. For the past decade, he had tried to live a life of absolute calm. At first, this meant staying at home for almost the entirety of the day, watching candles' flame burn, slowly melting the wax. He would always buy the same candles over and over—he knew which ones would have a calming effect on him.

Jasmine, the owner of the flower shop, was his only friend during the five years he relegated himself to his home. Every time he would come into the store, she knew that he wanted a candle. He bought it and left. No further words were exchanged.

Hans also enjoyed bonsai trimming. The trees were so petite, yet they stood so regally inside his house.

One time, a bonsai took Hans a whole year to trim. Each time, he would cut a fraction of an inch off one of the branches, swearing to himself that it would be the last time. And yet, he would come back the next day, stare at the branch, and decide that the tree wasn't ready to be given the title of being complete.

His life dragged on like this every single day. But he was fine with it.

Hans hated surprises. Thinking back on it, the day Jasmine knocked on his door did not deserve to be a day unlike any other. As usual, he sat on his sofa and trimmed a bonsai tree. Though he had a television in his living room, he only turned it on when he wanted to doze off to some soothing classical music.

The silence that day was broken by the rapping of knuckles on his mahogany door. No one had ever knocked on his door before. Hans did not think anyone cared enough to visit him.

Terrified of who could be behind the door, he stopped his bonsai trimming and sat without making any sound or movement. He was so still he could barely hear his own breath, each one hanging in the air like a drip of water ready to ripple a perfectly-still surface.

"Hans?" Jasmine's voice rang out in the silence. Hans did not respond. Jasmine's voice was unmistakable. "Hans, I know you're in there." He hoped she would give up and walk away. A glance at his bonsai tree told him that it wasn't finished. If only he had more time.

"For five years now, you've been sulking away in your house," Jasmine continued. "Did you think I wouldn't notice?" There was a pause. "Hans, it's me, Jasmine. Don't make me open the door myself."

Hans did not know how to react to this threat. He stood up from his couch and slowly approached the door, making sure his steps couldn't be heard. Evidently, he took too long.

Jasmine murmured, "*Qulf otvoren.*" Hans' lock clicked, and the door swung open. He reeled back. His eyes met Jasmine's.

Though she wasn't very tall, Jasmine's small stature seemed to fill up the doorway. She had unkempt hair and wore heart-shaped glasses. Her outfit was often composed of paint-splattered overalls with an apron over them spelling "Jasmine's Flower Shop." The apron had a little pocket for a beautiful pink rose to stick out of.

The various landscape paintings strung around Jasmine's flower shop explained the splotches of paint on her overalls. Though the scenery stretching beyond Brumont wasn't very interesting, Jasmine found a way to spruce it up in her depictions. And now she stood in Hans' doorway.

"What are you doing here?" he cried out.

Jasmine didn't answer his question. Her gaze meandered around his living room until she said, "It smells of hermit in here." As she looked back at Hans, a smile lit up on her face.

"Hans, I've been observing you for *a little bit* of time now," she said sarcastically, pinching her fingers in the air. "You get your candles and crawl back into his hole, huh? Poor thing. You live *here*?"

Hans' house wasn't messy. He made sure to keep it tidy, with his floor free of crumbs, his books lined up in height order on his bookshelves, and the bonsai trees deemed completed, standing like a military unit on his overhead shelves. He knew it wasn't how his house looked that annoyed Jasmine.

"You look as Scandinavian as ever, Hans. Your beard looks almost as perfect as those little bonsai trees I see over there. But you're just as untalkative, aren't you?"

"What do you want, Jasmine?" Hans asked.

Jasmine continued, "I want you to get out of this little hellhole you've dug your way into. You can't live like this."

"You couldn't care less for five years. Why did you come now?"

"Couldn't care less? You don't go outside, and you talk to no one. It has been painful to watch you hide yourself away like this. Please accept my help, Hans."

Hans took a deep breath. "What do you want me to do?"

"Get a job," Jasmine offered plainly.

Hans looked down at the floor. He knew that Jasmine was right. Though he found comfort in his monotonous life, a feeling that something was missing had recently begun to brew inside him. Ever since he finished his service as a special agent in the MCIA, he had tried to avoid the hectic life that he was once used to. The hectic life that now haunted him. Hans wanted every day to be like every other day so that his mind could finally rest.

Jasmine noticed the pensive look that clouded his face. "I'll leave you be," she said, gently shutting the door behind her as she left the house. Once outside, Jasmine murmured, "*Qulf blizu.*" The lock clicked. Hans was alone again.

He did not do any candle burning or bonsai trimming for the next three days. All he could do was lie down and think. Human interaction had gotten him into bad situations in the past. He was no longer a man of trust.

But for a while now, a little voice inside of Hans kept saying, "*You're useless.*" Over and over and over. A little voice that he knew, deep down, was correct. Was the bonsai trimming really therapeutic? Or was it a cowardly escape he'd indulged in until he reached some false perfection?

Jasmine came back three days after her first grand entrance, her knuckles rapping on the door just as they had done before. But Hans did not let her cast her lock opening spell. He approached the door, cracked it open, and looked down slightly to meet Jasmine's eyes.

"Are you ready?" Jasmine asked.

"I am," Hans said after a sigh.

He chose to be Brumont's stationmaster. The job was just as monotonous as his life had been before — the trains arrived every single day at the exact same time. The station at Brumont was small, and the trains were never late. The position had only been vacant for about a week. He was able to snag it.

To Jasmine, this was a victory. Greeting travelers, welcoming them to Brumont, and wishing them well on their way was like the "*Qulf otvoren*" to a man who had long sealed himself off from the world. It was the perfect job for Hans.

CHAPTER 3

Hans did not have long to linger in his memories. A whisper of voices returned him to the present—the men were coming out of the tree trunk to recollect him.

Lifting his head, Hans was yet again struck with brightness. The sun overhead made all the colors more vibrant but was equally as strenuous on the eyes.

The wind blew lightly. The weather was perfect. Paradise compared to the sharp winds and cloud-infested skies of Brumont, a northern town with abysmal conditions in the winter. That was one thing about Brumont that Hans didn't miss.

"So, Sleeping Beauty's awake?"

mocked one of the men.

"We're taking you inside," said another.

Hans was lifted off the ground. He could still feel the hat he wore every day as stationmaster on his head. It was impossible to tell how much time had passed since he was whisked away from Brumont. All he knew was that he still had his uniform on and that he had no clue where he was. Not a very useful combo of intelligence.

The men re-entered the tree trunk, this time hauling Hans behind them.

"We've got everything ready for you. We just want to ask you a few questions," said the man who Hans presumed to be the leader. Every time the men wanted to tell him something, this now-familiar voice would relay the message.

The men plopped Hans on a wooden stump, which was jutting out from the base of the wooden trunk. The seat was cool and rigid. For the moment, this was the pinnacle of comfort.

Hans took a moment to look around the room inside the tree trunk. There was something eerily ordinary about it—it felt just like any normal house. The only difference was the walls, which were made of wood. They were decorated by messy vines hanging from the ceiling and paintings half-concealed by the vines. The paintings were either portraits of the men and their families or landscapes that depicted stunning locations that reminded him of Earth.

In the corner was tucked away a kitchen, with foods Hans didn't recognize strewn across the counter. There was none of the technology that he was used to—no refrigerator or microwave. Instead, an open cabinet with unmelting frost told him that the men must've employed a similar strategy to keep their food cold as they did to bind his limbs. *Magic.*

A half-eaten sandwich lay on the counter. Or, at least, Hans guessed that it was a sandwich. The structure seemed similar to any sandwich he might eat for lunch, but the ingredients weren't quite the same. In the middle was a leaf like the ones growing on the tree trunk they had just crossed and meat with a sky-blue glimmer that the animals of this world gave off. Surrounding the ingredients was bread, composed of small seeds stuck together with a honey-like substance.

Looking outside the sole window of the room, through which a holy column of light shone, Hans saw a small garden on the side of the mountain with plants growing the seeds used in the sandwich.

"How resourceful," he thought.

As the men entered the room, they spread themselves out in the tight space. One man leaned against a railing, behind which stairs led down into rooms Hans knew he would never get to explore. Another man took off his suit jacket, placed it on another wooden stump, and sat down wearily, placing his head in his hand. The man Hans had labeled as the leader approached the kitchen and finished the sandwich.

"Did they take a snack break before dragging me in here?" he wondered.

"Oh, I can't do this anymore, Percival," complained the man sitting on the stump, addressing the head honcho. As he raised his head and took off his sunglasses, Hans saw that the man's eyes were a brilliant purple.

"Lucan, what do you want me to do? The guardian decided we had to go and capture this chump," Percival replied, motioning towards Hans. "You know what happened the last time anyone disobeyed him." Now that they were inside the trunk, the men seemed to drop the intimidating, uptight demeanor they had displayed earlier.

"I know, I know. You sound like a broken record, Perci."

"And you sound like my six-year-old," Percival jeered back.

"You know he's right, Perci," said the man standing near the staircase, also taking off his sunglasses. His eyes were orange.

"Every time we go to that stupid Earth, my eyes burn. Even through the glasses." He tossed them aside.

"Emrys, you think my eyes are any better than yours?" Percival asked. Though his glasses looked the same as Lucan and Emrys', Percival winced at the light when he took them off. After taking a moment to recover, Hans could see that Percival's eyes were baby blue. "We just do what the guardian tells us to do and go home to our families."

"Viviana can't stand this anymore. Our last journey to Earth almost got us killed. I came home with half my life force gone and had to take three months off. You remember, right, Emrys?" Lucan asked, hopefully waiting for an answer. Emrys nodded.

"Yeah, I know that the guardian has goals much bigger than us. But I don't know how much longer Clarine will let me go act on his whims," said Emrys. Looking at Hans, he continued, "And this time, it's all because of you."

Hans had been invested while listening in on the men's conversation. Now that the attention was turned towards him, he wasn't quite as into it.

"You didn't think we forgot about you, did you?" Percival demanded. He walked towards a cabinet, opened it, and pulled out a file with "Hans Eindride" scrawled on the cover. He flipped through the leaves of paper in the file until he stopped on a page, staring at it for a moment.

"The guardian always gives us one of these when he has a target for us. And they usually make complete sense to me. But there's this one thing in your file that I don't quite understand," Percival continued.

Hans finally spoke. "Who are you?"

"Ah. So he is able to talk," said Emrys.

"Ha. And we thought that we took his tongue off when we snatched him," laughed Lucan.

"Who are *we*? We're kind of like *you*, Hans," said Percival, throwing the open file at Hans' feet. Hans looked down, seeing the page with his occupational history open. A section noted that he now worked as a stationmaster. They knew enough about him to be up to date.

But Percival seemed to be focused on something else. He demanded, "The special forces for the MCIA? The guardian never told us what the MCIA was. May you please enlighten us?"

"Why should I tell you? What do you want from me?" replied Hans.

"Oh, I was just curious. You don't have to tell me if you don't want to." Percival approached Lucan, whispered something into his ear, and then walked towards Hans, looming over him. Lucan, upon hearing Percival's words, descended the stairs that he had been leaning over, disappearing into the depths of the tree.

"I'm sorry. I almost forgot to answer your second question, Hans. You had something precious to our peoples, and the guardian told us we could use any means necessary to get it back," said Percival, gesturing towards Emrys.

Next to Emrys, a bag was slumped against the stump that he was sitting on. He reached into the bag and pulled out the heathers that the men had confiscated from Hans' booth. Immediately after taking the flowers out, the room was filled with an enchanting scent. The flowers were as perky as usual. Hans had guessed correctly that magic was involved.

Percival continued, "You see, there's a special ceremony that happens once every five years. Without its proper completion, we all slowly decay till death. That's what our tradition says, at least. And it's best not to play with tradition." Percival crouched down in front of Hans, roughly bringing himself to Hans' eye level.

"I have no clue how you got a hold of these flowers. Last time I checked, they were only grown in the guardian's private garden. And we *kind of* need them for the ceremony."

"They're the most important part," Emrys interrupted.

"Yeah, what he said."

"Well, you've got your flowers. Can I go now?" Hans asked, though he knew what the answer would be. Both men laughed.

"Let you go? Hans Eindride, you've committed treason of the highest order. You've sabotaged the lives of everyone in Charthosk by taking away the guardian's holy white heathers. I sent my buddy Lucan over there to bring out a special weapon. We're merciful, after all. We, the special forces of this land's sacred guardian, will kill you painlessly," Percival declared, grinning. The glare of his charming baby-blue eyes pierced Hans' soul.

Percival's words made Hans shudder. He knew that there was only one way to save himself from this situation, but it pained him that he was forced to employ it. Hans lowered his head, taking deep breaths.

"Well, your biggest mistake was sending that guy downstairs," Hans murmured.

"Huh? Look at me when you're talking," Percival demanded.

Hans raised his head, making eye contact with Percival. Percival looked closer at Hans, his face scrunched up in confusion. His investigation didn't take very long. He staggered back until he reached the kitchen counter.

Puzzled, Emrys asked, "Perci, what's wrong? Are you scared of this small fry or something?"

"May I ask one question before you end me?" interjected Hans. His eyes were locked with Percival's. Percival's breathing became heavier as his panic grew in intensity.

"Speak," he said.

"What type of meat do you have there in your sandwich?"

Emrys laughed heartily. He answered, "What silly final words. It's a kiyik. Similar to a deer in your world." Emrys' laugh broke the stare between Hans and Percival. They both shifted their gaze towards Emrys.

He stood up from his stump, placing the heathers carefully on top of it. Turning to look at Hans, Emrys froze. His smile dropped.

"Perci, his eyes are green."

"A kiyik, you say?" repeated Hans.

Percival stepped forward. "No. I won't let you. *Shamol kolona perverti*," he roared, his face filled with fear and his voice filled with rage.

Percival got into a fighting stance, setting his left foot in front while placing most of his weight on his right foot. He put his right hand behind his back while raising his left, extending it so it was aimed at Hans' throat.

Both the window and the door were forced open by intense winds, which Hans could feel entering the room and swirling around Percival's arm.

"Too late," said Hans, chanting, "*Ildiz blokada*."

As soon as Percival's gathering winds finished accumulating, they shot out towards Hans' neck. The column of wind felt like a storm, so powerful that Hans could see its shape. It looked like a spear aimed at him — wind that had gathered in a disciplined formation, capped off with a deadly point.

Percival's typhoon was fast. Unfortunately for him, Hans' defense was faster.

As the wind column shot forward from Percival's hand, a colossal root sprouted up from the ground, intercepting the attack. The root completely destroyed the comfortable abode nestled in the tree, which swayed gently. Now, there was quite a magnificent centerpiece the men probably wouldn't appreciate.

Hans noticed how powerful Percival was. Looking straight ahead, he could see the hole that Percival's wind had bored through the thick root. He was staring at Percival through the hole, who suddenly fell to the floor.

Percival had used a three-word attack

right from the start, aiming to bring an immediate end to Hans. However, a three-word attack also meant tremendous fatigue. As Percival wearily got to his feet, he desperately began preparing another attack.

Suddenly, purple smoke began to creep its way from the floor below. Noticing the smoke, Hans began to chant another spell. He decided to go with his magnum opus: "*Ajoyib zverski kontrole.*" Nothing happened immediately after Hans' incantation. That was not its purpose.

Hans heard steps up the stairs. It seemed the root that had bent itself out of shape from below the tree interrupted whoever was below. *Lucan.*

Immediately following his steps up, Lucan chanted, "*Lablar zapecacena,*" ready to aid his teammates above.

Hans had anticipated this spell. The smoke lifted itself off the ground and moved towards his mouth. He tried to back away, but his back bumped into the wall behind him. Hans hopelessly tried to shoo away the smoke. It accumulated around his mouth and clasped down, preventing him from speaking. There was one important rule that Hans had been taught in terms of magic--it cannot be formed without words.

It was a classy trick for Lucan to go straight for Hans' ability to speak. But Hans smiled despite his predicament. The spell he had just invoked would prove very handy.

Emrys, who had been watching all the chaos unfold, pulled himself together and joined Percival and Lucan in attacking Hans. He began to cast his incantation too, saying, "*Tosh—*"

Suddenly, an animal jumped through the window, which was still ajar after Percival's winds tore it open. It was a kiyik, barreling straight towards Emrys.

"A kiyik?" Emrys directed his focus towards the animal that was jumping at him, finishing his incantation, "*—udarac.*" A boulder ripped itself off the cliffside and hurtled through the window, intercepting the kiyik.

The animal was certainly majestic. Its horns were much larger than that of a deer — Hans could tell that the one he had called to protect him was a male kiyik. The sky-blue glimmer was glamorous on a creature this large, much more so than the tiny rodent he had seen before. The pattern on its side was simple, but Hans knew that if he looked closer, he would see a world of intricacy. He couldn't understand how nature could create something this beautiful.

But he didn't have time to let his mind wander. Hans had a battle to focus on.

He had figured that since the men were resourceful with most parts of the sandwich that Percival had eaten, they would be resourceful with the meat, too. That glimmer that Hans had seen peek through the canopy was just as he had suspected — an animal that he would be able to take control of. Thankfully, there was a kiyik close enough for Hans to call to his aid.

No, not a kiyik. A herd of kiyik.

Another kiyik jumped through the

open door, prancing its way towards Lucan. Lucan flipped open a pocketknife and started slashing at the kiyik. It seemed that he did not have any offensive magic in his arsenal. Though it looked like Lucan had the upper hand against the kiyik with his knife, the distraction was more important to Hans. Lucan's loss of concentration also meant the spell he had cast earlier lost its effect. Hans could speak again.

As Emrys turned his attention back towards Hans, Hans stared him in the eyes, saying, "*Tok zapeltjati katastrofa.*" The vines hanging from the ceiling began to entangle themselves, crawling around Emrys' appendages. As the vines grew in volume, they became solid and hard to move in.

Emrys tried to get himself out with another spell, but the vines started moving around his throat and slowly choked the air out of him. As his eyes closed and he fell into a state of unconsciousness, the vines finished moving, creating a perfect net strung around Emrys' limp body. It felt like an altar to Mother Nature, with Emrys as the sacrifice.

The men found themselves very unlucky. They had instigated a battle with a foe who was in his perfect environment — a mancapableofcontrollingnaturesurrounded by the wilderness. With animals prancing around in the woods and a home situated on the inside of a tree trunk, Hans was not at a disadvantage. And his experience with magic meant he could cast three-word spells much more easily than Percival, who still hadn't fully recovered from the powerful gust he had created earlier.

Hans was certainly not exhausted. He had done this before.

But, when he looked down at his hands, they were trembling intensely. He clasped them together, hoping to calm himself down. He took a moment to listen to his breath, observing the chaos that had found a home in the once-peaceful tree trunk abode.

Hans, yet again, backed up against the

wall behind him. His breathing was harsh and inconsistent—he had grown panicked, and he could barely control his cascading emotions.

He wished he wasn't here in Charthosk. He wished Jasmine had never taken him out of his home. He wished that he could get back on his couch and continue building his humble collection of bonsai trees. He told himself, *"I have to finish this and get out of here,"* wishing that fighting wouldn't be the only way to end this conflict.

Lucan tore Hans away from his thoughts. Diverting his gaze towards him, Hans realized Lucan had finished sparring with the kiyik he had sent. He regretted not summoning a larger army to his aid. The kiyik lay on the ground, its legs sprayed out, motionless. Lifeless. Hans did not have time to apologize.

The kiyik had fought valiantly. Its horns weren't as large as the one who had entered the tree before, signaling to Hans that this one was female. He wondered whether his abilities made him tear apart kiyik families. Glancing at Lucan, he noticed the deep slash that the kiyik had left on his body before being overpowered. Hans remembered his powers made nature pledge complete loyalty to him. For once, he felt sorry. Sorry for the kiyik and its children, who were now completely alone.

Lucan, too, had a miserable look on his face. He looked away from the kiyik, taking deep breaths to stabilize himself after his struggle with one of nature's beasts. He quickly regained his demeanor and charged at Hans. He had a job to do, after all.

Lucan clearly compensated for his lack of offensive magic with his physical attributes. His speed startled Hans, who readied himself for whatever Lucan would do with his pocketknife.

Lucan slashed from Hans' left. Hans thought the slash to be sloppy, intercepting it with a block and moving towards Lucan, his elbow aimed at Lucan's face. He got a clean hit. Lucan staggered back.

Hans could see blood trickling down from Lucan's nose. Lucan didn't seem to notice. He went low with his knife this time. Hans didn't have as much time to react and was slashed in his abdomen. He immediately felt searing pain. He winced and clutched his stomach. His vision momentarily became blurry.

Lucan took the opportunity to hook Hans in the face. Hans ducked under it and kicked Lucan's knee. Lucan lost his balance and fell backwards. As he hastily pulled himself up, Hans cried out, "*Kemiruvchi okrsaj.*"

A light pitter-patter could be heard outside of the trunk. As it approached the men inside, the pitter-patter became louder and louder. Squeaks added themselves to the cacophony of noises.

Lucan got distracted by the sounds that were rapidly approaching him. Little rodents jumped at his feet, making him lose his balance. There were hundreds of them now attempting to pile through the door, stacking themselves on top of Lucan. He couldn't attack when he was in the presence of such cute critters. And he certainly couldn't attack if they were trapping his arms and legs under their combined weight.

"*Chaqmoq udarac.*" As Lucan tried to wrestle the rodents he now found himself struggling against, Percival finally got himself to his feet and mustered the energy to summon a spell.

Hans' head pivoted, catching a glimpse of Percival's arm yet again extended and pointing at him. Percival was motionless, staring straight down his arm at Hans as if he were staring down the scope of a rifle. His attack was still taking time to build up.

Hans' instincts told him to roll backwards, avoiding whatever Percival was planning. Right as he did so, Percival finished his accumulation of charge. Lightning shot out from his hand, barely missing Hans. Instead, it hit the wall behind him, leaving the trunk sizzling hot. It hadn't been powerful enough to start a fire, but Hans noticed one of the family pictures that had been hanging on the wall was now eerily missing.

As Percival put up his other arm to summon more lightning, Hans retaliated, "*Barg skretanje.*" A branch emerged from the ground, with a massive leaf growing seemingly out of nowhere. The leaf deflected Percival's arm, making his lightning hit the ceiling. The entirety of the tree shuddered.

Percival was going all out on his attacks. He was wasting energy, hoping for any chance to take Hans out in one shot. He tried to put his arm up again, but two more branches sprouted up, leaves gently wrapping around him. He didn't have enough left in him to fight back.

Turning his attention back to Lucan, Hans shooed away the rodents he had summoned. They hadn't done a lot of damage to Lucan, but they were enough of a nuisance that he was out of energy, too.

Hans said very simply, "*Uyqu.*" Since

Lucan was so tired, Hans could just use sleep magic to lull him into a peaceful slumber.

The smoke that Lucan had summoned earlier, which still lingered on the floor, now pulled itself away from Hans and crept towards Lucan, slowly covering his eyes. Lucan's breaths became heavier, and his drowsy consciousness was now in a different realm.

Hans was on the verge of collapse. His adrenaline was still at a high and his body made him feel like he could take down the entirety of Charthosk. But his mind was playing games with him.

Looking around the trunk that he had just fought a hard-won victory in, all Hans saw was absolute disarray. The root he had summoned still occupied the center of the trunk. The hole Percival bored through it remained like an honor of the highest order. A boulder lay next to the window, the only source of light in the dimly lit room. The pot of heathers still stood regally on the tree stump, miraculously unaffected by the chaos.

Emrys dangled from vines, which had formed a labyrinth around his arms and legs. Lucan slept, his train of thought now possessed by dreams and nightmares. The deer carcass he had slain sprawled itself next to him, though its train of thought no longer ran. Regret filled the deepest cracks of Hans' mind.

A sharp pain reminded him that he was not in the best shape himself. He tried to pull himself together to deal with the last man standing. Though he did his best to act like he was okay, he couldn't hide his limp as he approached Percival. Percival put up his arm to keep Hans at bay, but it immediately collapsed.

In between ragged breaths, Percival asked the question that had occupied his mind since the moment he saw Hans' eyes. "You're the Terror of the Forest, aren't you?"

"That's what they call me, huh?"

"How dare you come back to Charthosk?" Percival yelled out, exasperated.

"You people from Earth don't belong here. We were all so thankful when we heard the Terror finally went away." Percival paused. He took a moment to examine Hans. "*You*. My friends were in Celesmond as you watched it torn to the ground."

"Are you forgetting that *you* brought me here?" Hans cut in, motioning to the destroyed room. A blank stare filled Percival's face. His eyes were filled with dread. He had realized what he'd done. Percival collapsed to the ground.

"The MCIA was the Magic Containment and Investigation Administration," Hans continued. "My grandfather was the founder. I was his most loyal agent. He sent me on missions all throughout Charthosk. He said it was to explore this magical world. All that came of it was atrocity. I..." Hans couldn't continue. He had been reminded of his past. The past he had so desperately tried to escape. Everything that Hans had gotten involved in during his time in Charthosk had ended up like the room he now stood in. Chaos. Pain. Destruction.

Hans had run away from it all. His last mission was to Celesmond, which his grandfather ended up destroying. "Mission" was the most extreme euphemism Hans had ever heard. This "mission" was the first time it hit him that his loyalty to his grandfather had harmed a world full of life.

Standing back in Charthosk, haunted by his past and now haunted by the present, the name Percival had called him rang in Hans' ears. *Terror of the Forest. Terror of the Forest.* Hans did not want to be called the Terror of the Forest. His decisions didn't give him a choice.

Percival looked up at Hans. Tears were coming down his eyes. Hans could feel it—regret filled the deepest cracks of Percival's mind, too.

Here were two regretful men staring at each other in a Charthoskian tree trunk. Hans had to get away. He couldn't let himself impart any more harm on a land he should never have been in.

Percival blurted out, "Please, don't hurt anyone. Please," he called out desperately.

Hans approached Percival. A single tear rolled down his face. "I'm sorry" was all he said as he jammed his palm right at Percival's chin, cleanly knocking him out.

Hans collapsed to his knees. He felt a throbbing pain from the wound Lucan had delivered. He tore off part of his clothes and wrapped it around his abdomen, lying down to ease the pain. His stationmaster uniform was no more. He yearned to be back in his humble cabin.

Hans was trapped in a world where even he, a capable user of nature magic, couldn't access healing powers. All residents of Charthosk had it locked away from their magical arsenal. The only person he'd ever seen accomplish healing was his grandfather. It was a shame how cynical his view of Charthosk had been. It was an even deeper shame that he had used his powers, with the MCIA behind him, to wreak havoc, not heal and nurture.

Hans knew Charthosk well. He had long heard about the festival that occurred every five years — the peoples of Charthosk threw sacrifices into a boiling pot to save the land from eternal ruin and decay. The core of the ceremony was the sacrifice of the current guardian and the selection of a new one.

Though he heard the stories of these rituals, which were deeply engraved in the history of Charthosk, Hans had never been able to attend a festival himself. His grandfather had never let him. But he knew that it was his best chance to get back to Brumont.

Hans' destination was the Crossroads, a central village in Charthosk that housed inhabitants of all three existing factions: the Earth Guild, Sky Crusaders, and Chaos Harbingers. Though the factions needed each other, they rarely intermingled.

The festival was the only time the

populations of the peaceful factions were brought together to celebrate their peace. The ceremony, which brought about the next guardian and appeased the gods, was crucial not only to the culture of Charthosk but also to its survival.

Hans understood why the men were so adamant about getting the heathers back. What he found odd was that he had never heard of the heathers being one of the sacrifices.

Hans didn't know how he would find the Crossroads, as he had no way to orient himself in the dense tree labyrinth called the Gentle Thicket. Though it didn't present much danger to any brave souls who traveled through it, it was the ultimate test of patience and perseverance. It seemed futile to try to traverse. Hans prepared for the journey anyway.

He found a cloak hanging above the staircase that led down into the depths of the trunk. For a second, he considered exploring but was motivated against it by his wish to leave.

Hans pulled the cloak over his shoulders, put on the sunglasses that Percival had thrown aside so that no one could see his bland, brown eyes, and slipped the heathers under the cloak. He had to figure out their significance — *why did these men have to suffer?*

Hans was ready. He stepped outside, greeted yet again by the startlingly beautiful weather. A light breeze blew his cloak's hood down.

No, he wasn't ready. Gazing out into the beauty of Charthosk, a beauty he had never given himself time to genuinely take in, he began to ask himself if he deserved to stand in this realm with his head held so high. Though he had recovered physically, since his wound wasn't deep enough to cause him continuing harm, his body reached out and stroked his mind, telling him not to move.

Hans didn't want to go towards the Crossroads, wherever it was. He didn't want

to meet any other inhabitants of Charthosk —
he was terrified they would all look at him
in fear. He didn't want to face the people
whom he had wronged. He didn't want to
live a life of turmoil anymore.

Hans looked down at his hands. They
were trembling just as much as they had
been before. His breath got shakier. He sat
himself down, his efforts of calming himself
in vain.

Now, doubt was closing in like a lion,
leisurely moving through the grass, knowing
its prey couldn't run away. Guilt panged
like a bite from the lion — an antelope's leg
caught in the snare of the lion's majestic
mouth. Shame encircled the carcass of Hans'
past like vultures, ready to feast on a man
who no longer believed that he deserved to
take up the same air that Percival, Lucan, or
Emrys took up — men with families, goals,
and communities to come back to when
they finished their toils for the guardian of
Charthosk.

No, Hans was alone. All he had were

worms looming over him, crawling up through the ground to fill the emptiness the vultures of shame had left behind. He lay down and closed his eyes. Tears did not let themselves flow. He was helpless, his face just like his pride—a parched riverbed licking its lips, scrounging for a drop of water.

Suddenly, a loud sound snapped Hans away from the reclusion in his thoughts. He sat up and looked around. The loud sound was followed by a flash of light to his right, a brilliant firework that he knew was made with magic. Two more lit up the sky. Each of their patterns was unique. The way they filled the sky was a masterpiece.

The fireworks were clearly preparation for the festival. Almost autonomously, Hans' body got itself up and put on the cloak's hood. His legs, now possessing a mind of their own, took one step after another in the direction of the fireworks. The Crossroads was his only hope.

CHAPTER 4

Hans had walked a long way to get to his destination. Each step felt foreign and the Crossroads even more so. As he approached the town, he heard voices growing in volume, pouring into the dense forest.

Hans didn't encounter any animals on his expedition to the Crossroads. It hadn't been particularly difficult—though he had to scale down the mountain from the tree trunk, his journey had been a simple exercise in walking in one direction.

Now, Hans stood before a massive, magnificent red gate marking the entrance to the isolated town. It had brightly-colored lanterns hanging off of it. Looking up at the gate, he noticed that the lights were the same color as the Gentle Thicket's leaves—sky-blue, orange, and purple tones illuminated the ground.

Hans' hand instinctively crept up to his hood, making sure it was firmly over his head. His vision was still obscured by the tinted sunglasses. He hoped his eyes were just as obscured. He took a deep breath and entered the town.

The Crossroads was populated by a festival like no other. Hans entered into a main road with no trees blocking the sunlight. A sole tree stood at the center of the town, larger than any of the trees in the forest, looming over the Crossroads.

Even through his sunglasses, Hans could tell how bright the day was. The whole town functioned like a festive organ, the marketplace a loud and lively beating heart.

All Hans saw down the entirety of the road were people. Of course, they were nothing like the people of Brumont—

the citizens of each faction could easily be distinguished by their features.

Many of the Sky Crusaders had little wings peeking out of the back of their shirts. Their eyes were baby blue, just like Percival's. Each person had unique hair — various shades of blue sitting on their heads. Most of their clothes were loose and free.

Hans saw two Crusader kids run past him, giggling. A smile poked itself onto his face. The energy of the kids was even greater than the energy he felt surrounding him. They both wore brown dresses, which were long, simple, and barely hanging onto their shoulders as they plowed through the crowd. Each of their steps was light, their flats barely touching the ground. One of them had gorgeous earrings — little, smiling clouds.

Hans was able to catch a glimpse of the girls' backs as they slipped into an alley. They had barely visible wings.

It was Sky Crusader tradition that whoever grew full wings would be revered in their society. Wings were a sign of the blessing of the Sky. Other adults, most of whom couldn't fly, would find themselves the target of nature's scorn. These girls were not among the blessed few.

Behind the two Crusader girls ran another girl, her dress colored a shade of navy blue. She was part of the Earth Guild. Her hair was orange, and her eyes were gloomy yellow. Her dress wasn't as simple or free as the dresses of the girls she was chasing. The dress had an intricate pattern sewn into it and was tied tightly around the girl's torso. She wasn't wearing any shoes, so each step left a footprint in the unpaved road.

Hans figured that the girls were friends who didn't get many opportunities to see each other. They were now playing tag in matching dresses. As the Earth girl ran, she grabbed a handful of chips from one of the stalls without the vendor noticing. Giggling, she, too, slipped into the alley, disappearing from his view. He chuckled at the girl's stealth.

Hans heard a hearty laugh to his right. Pivoting away from the game of tag he had glimpsed, he saw two Earth Guild and two Sky Crusader men standing in a small circle, engaged in a lively conversation.

Guilders were not as blessed by nature as Crusaders. The whole mantra of the Earth Guild was grit—Guilders found their way up through their society through hard work.

The men standing in the circle had rocks strewn across their backs as if they were wearing armor. Though they did not glisten, Hans knew that the rocks trained the strength of the men who adorned them. The strongest of the Earth Guild were often highly respected.

As Hans pushed his way through the crowd, he remembered that each elemental group was limited to their element—each Charthoksian resident could only have one of the three elements that existed in the world. Many, including his grandfather, had long tried to investigate the reason why. None had come to a conclusion. Everyone just had to live by the rules of the world.

Hans' thoughts were interrupted by an unignorable aroma. He had wandered closer to the center of the town, where the main marketplace was at its busiest. This part of the town reminded him that the Crossroads was not built for residency. It was more like one massive tourist trap, ready to pounce on any unsuspecting visitor.

Vendors shouted into the crowd, begging weary travelers to take a look at their goods. People constantly flowed through the streets, chatting with their buddies, approaching stalls, and observing what new recipes had popped up in the last five years.

The dishes were vibrant in color, smell, and, Hans presumed, flavor. He noticed a tray with the chips that the girl had grabbed earlier. As the vendor was distracted by someone buying a blue rib of meat, Hans grabbed a chip and slipped it into his mouth. As he chewed, he disappeared into the center of the crowd. The chip tasted dry and salty, but a tangy citrus flavor had been added to compensate. He enjoyed the remainder of the chip.

The crowd moved as if powered by a raging furnace. Someone pushed Hans, bumping him into another person. He apologized and looked down, searching for a place to escape the crowd. He slipped into a tavern he had spotted and crept into a corner without anyone noticing him.

The atmosphere of the tavern was just as lively as the hustle and bustle of the people outside. The bar was packed. A Crusader man with almost invisible wings shyly took a shot of a clear liquid. Another man, whose faction Hans struggled to catch because of how vigorously the man chugged down drinks, was sweating and rambling deliriously. Even the bartender acknowledged that the man had drunk too much.

Hans scanned the room. He told

himself he didn't have to fear being found out—people were so caught up in their conversations.

"At least they're happy," Hans thought, allowing himself to let loose in the spirited environment. Charthosk seemed to be just fine without any Terror of the Forest roaming around.

As he took a deep breath to steady himself amid the hectic tavern, he noticed a group of people wearing purple in the opposite corner.

They were Chaos Harbingers. Their capital, Vilemere, was the core of the Charthoskian higher education system, with major scholars from all three lands accumulating there to do research. And it drew almost as many tourists as the Crossroads with its promise of innovation. It was safe to say that the residents lived lavishly.

The Harbingers sitting in the corner bore the emblem of the central Vilemere University. They seemed suspicious to Hans in the hushed way they talked and looked around.

"*I'm not one to talk,*" he reminded himself.

These Harbingers had luscious locks of dark purple hair and eyes of a lavish and playful shade of magenta. They had simple outfits—a beige sweater vest on top of a white button-down, sharply ironed black dress pants, and a plum-purple robe regally draped over their shoulders. They had little horns sitting on their heads and varying sizes of tails stretching from their lower backs. One Harbinger man had a lanky tail that rested gently around the chair that he sat on. Another had a thick tail that he held in his arms and caressed as he spoke to his friends around the table.

Hans started to feel nostalgia for Charthosk. At one time, he could be a part of its culture. Though just an observer—a fisherman calmly sitting on his boat rocking gently in the waves—he had fond memories of his initial time in Charthosk. But at one point or another, the fisherman must throw the reel in and hook an unassuming trout. A fisherman is a fisherman, after all—the waves were his domain and the catch his objective.

At some points, Hans wished he was in the water too. There would've been nothing wrong with being a fish in a vast ocean, a commonality in a constellation of life. But he no longer had to worry about his involvement in Charthosk.

"Perhaps they don't remember me at all," Hans told himself. This thought was rapidly broken by a loud voice coming from the center of the tavern—a Harbinger man sat on a table in everyone's view.

"Let me tell you a story," he proudly announced, turning all attention towards him.

The man looked like what Hans imagined a king's bard would look like. He wore shoes pointed at the tip and pants that poofed out halfway down his thighs. His shirt was regal and had a striped design. It was cuffed at his forearms and bore an emblem of one of Vilemere's lower universities. He wore a headband right up to his horns to keep back his long, flowing purple hair.

The man spoke loud and clear, signaling to Hans that he was a frequent orator. The people in the tavern, for whom this didn't seem uncommon, gathered around the bard-like man. Hans moved in, too, so as not to seem suspicious. His curiosity had been piqued.

"Who here is ready for the story of a lifetime?" the man asked. He was met with awkward silence.

"We're not kids, man," a Guilder shouted out from the crowd, raising a slight chuckle from the anticipating people.

"Sorry, working with kids really gets to you sometimes. It's nice being able to tell a story at the Crossroads once in a while." He added sarcastically, "Kids, am I right?" There was a murmur of agreement. The man recollected himself, took a moment to raise the suspense hanging in the tense air, and continued.

"In a land where we have three magical elements—the rough Earth, the heavenly Sky, and the mysterious Chaos," he said, confidently looking around, "the existence of a fourth element was a surprise to the people of Charthosk. In a system no one had ever been able to beat and which has given researchers nightmares, who could possibly be… different?

"A man capable of controlling Nature sat among us for decades, an unknown devil, before suddenly disappearing after igniting a conflict in Celesmond…" Hans anticipated the next words. He stared at the man, wishing they had never come out of his thin-lipped mouth. "The Terror of the Forest."

A murmur rose in the crowd. Some people stopped paying attention and restarted conversations with their companions. They seemed to have heard this story before, a recounting of what Hans had done. Like listening to a broken record, they were no longer interested.

Hans lost interest, too. He didn't want to hear how he was perceived. How the name "Terror of the Forest" became tied to him. Born from the actions of his past, the story was told and retold—Hans imagined other taverns where this was the talk of the town, where crowds looked down on him with unvoiced judgment.

Hans tried to get away. To get up and escape the tavern. But he was crippled in his seat. The storyteller caught everyone's attention again with his charismatic voice, and the story went on.

"He's a man with green eyes. Rumors say his eyes are terrifying, even to the strongest Guilder. I have never seen the pierce of those pupils, which many have described as similar to a burgut." A bird. A terrifyingly large bird whose glare freezes prey.

"I am thankful. The Terror has the magic of a god—the power to control life itself. Stories have said he has the stamina of a stallion, can cast three-word spells on a fleeting whim, and holds the loyalty of all animals big and small. Celesmond experienced it all firsthand. We must hope he does not awaken from his slumber. We must hope the Terror never spreads any further."

The man was an incredible storyteller. His voice put a stop to the chugs of even the excessively drunk man at the bar, whose liver was probably begging for mercy. They had probably never heard it told this beautifully before, but the story was clear, and the message was simple—Hans should be feared.

"Fear him," the storyteller confirmed, "for Celesmond didn't, and they paid. The first city where two factions lived together. Tried to thrive together. But the Terror of the Forest didn't approve. Just weeks after it finished construction and people were getting used to life, it was all over in hours. Nature turned against the citizens of Celesmond. Animals rebelled. Trees uprooted themselves in absolute loyalty. By the end of that fateful day, it had been destroyed. We were at the mercy of a deity whom we had never seen. Who did not belong."

Hans barely heard the storyteller say that no one knew the true casualty count. At this point, he felt distant from his body. Words blurred, and thoughts crumbled.

Hans forced himself up and slipped out of the tavern. The storyteller was nearing the end of his story. He stopped his speech to look out at the opening of the tavern — the sudden movement had caught his eye. But Hans was gone. The bard-like man resumed.

CHAPTER 5

Hans had managed to escape the storyteller's carnivorous words. He looked down at his hands. They were shaking again. He could hear the distant roar of a vengeful train rolling on the tracks of reality. Was he hallucinating?

Hans yet again stood in the busy streets of the Crossroads. He looked up at the sky, which was beginning to fill with a palette of extraordinary colors. The sun was setting, and the cloudless day was turning to dusk.

It was becoming too dark for Hans to see with his sunglasses on. He slipped them off and lowered his head. Luck had to be on his side for his brown eyes to go unnoticed. He could try to pass for an Earth Guilder who just hadn't developed the brilliant hue in eye color many of the others had.

The festival was preparing for the next day when the ceremony would officially take place. Hans had to leave before it happened. His best chance was to go towards the massive tree at the center of the Crossroads, the home of the guardian, the Mammoth Oak.

At the base of the Mammoth Oak, a cauldron was set up, where Hans presumed the ceremony would take place.

The tree itself had a massive trunk, defended by the guardian's magic so that it would be impossible to topple. Its branches occupied the beautiful sunset-infested sky, with uniquely patterned leaves stretching out from the thickest branches to the thinnest twigs.

At the top of the tree, Hans noticed a narrow column of smoke billowing out and dispersing into the air. That was where the guardian lived. He didn't know how the guardian was chosen, how powerful he was, or if he would ever encounter him.

Hans could hear a commotion in the direction of the cauldron, where a platform had been set up. Looking up as discreetly as he could, he saw a gathering of people around the tree, anticipating something. He did not understand why this was happening now. The ceremony was still a day away. These people should've been enjoying the festivities of the Crossroads.

As Hans approached this central area — no one paying him any attention because of their interest in the cauldron — he heard a booming voice from someone who was ascending to the platform.

The voice belonged to a man wearing a navy-blue suit. Compared to the informal wear of everyone else around him, Hans presumed this was an official of the Crossroads, someone who would be administering the ceremony.

What struck him most about this man

was his fully developed wings — he was one of the blessed Sky Crusaders. He had also been chosen as the person to lead one of the most important ceremonies in Charthoskian culture. Nature's luck had been kind to him.

The man announced, "Good evening, ladies and gentlemen of Charthosk. My name is Felix. I will be leading tomorrow's ceremony. I know that all of you have been preparing well. The guardian is preparing, too, for his destined sacrifice. For centuries, we have depended on this ceremony to stop the decay that looms over us — a threat we can all feel. This cauldron that stands before me will be where we will complete the necessary sacrifice.

"At the moment, everything our tradition requires for the ceremony is ready. The heathers the guardian had requested are currently being searched for by our top special agents. I am currently in contact with Percival, our honorable Sky Crusader agent. He has been informing me that the apprehension of the thief of the heather flowers is going well," Felix explained.

Hans noticed a weakening of confidence in Felix's voice. He knew Percival would not be able to tell Felix anything at the moment. He peeked inside his cloak. He had been holding onto the heathers the whole time.

"But I come before you to announce that we have another sacrifice — from Earth, which had not too long ago tortured us with its Terror of the Forest," Felix said, gesturing to someone off the platform to bring something on. Hans didn't know what to expect.

Felix continued, "We bring another human from their cursed world. We confirmed the human isn't powerful enough to be the Terror. But, it is a way to appease the magic deities, who shape our world and give us the life which we struggle to understand."

Suddenly, a familiar smell overcame Hans. It made him feel like he was lying on a soft flower bed in a meadow of emptiness.

A meadow of absolute calm. It made him feel like he could lie down to rest and let his worries slip away.

Hans closed his eyes. He imagined flowers rising up from the bed. Roses poking his skin painlessly with their prickly stems. Daisies brushing his face with their petals. Tulips surrounding his ears, saving him from the world of endless sound that he lived in. The flowers pleasantly surrounded Hans. He had not felt this comfortable since coming to Charthosk.

This sensation nudged him into his memories. It reminded him of a little flower shop. A shop where one could buy candles that smelled like all kinds of flowers. A shop where beautiful paintings of Charthosk hung on the walls, impressing customers with views forever unknown to them. A shop where a short woman stood and welcomed you. Silently. With a big, open heart.

Hans opened his eyes to see the origin of the familiar smell. It was Jasmine. His memories had not deceived him. This was his friend, a fellow member of the MCIA, before the events in Celesmond made them both decide to leave Charthosk behind. The owner of Jasmine's Flower Shop, home of whatever little tourism Brumont offered.

Hans' ally stood on stage, completely involuntarily. She was brought on by a Guild man and a Crusader woman, directed towards the center of the platform by Felix.

There was a murmur among the crowd. They had noticed the mysterious smell, too.

Questions ran through Hans' mind. *"Why do they have Jasmine? Why is Jasmine producing this scent?"*

Jasmine was on stage, completely wrapped up. Her hands and feet were bound by a thick, tightly knotted rope. The rest of her body had one long rope wrapped around it, concealing almost everything. Her mouth had been sealed shut with a tape-like adhesive. Her eyes were closed as if she was unconscious. The smell indicated this wasn't as true as Felix might've hoped.

To Hans' knowledge, Jasmine was a powerful Nature user. How did she let herself get into this situation?

Felix began speaking again. "Tomorrow will be a special day for everyone as we make the prophesied sacrifice. But to end today off on a good note, we will throw this woman from Earth into the cauldron. Let our unseen deities rejoice!"

More people had begun to gather around the tree. Hans wanted to do something to save Jasmine, but he was completely powerless, squeezed on both sides by people excited to see the show. He would never be able to get through this mass of people who were observing a murder disguised as an appeasement of the gods.

Horror now emanated from the once-peaceful flower bed. The roses stung, and the daisies choked. Hans' mind was screaming but the tulips didn't let him hear his own cry. His voice echoed once, then disappeared.

The sacrifice would happen now, and he would have to watch, filled with nothing but fear.

Hans looked up at the tree. He wondered whether the guardian was watching any of this. What the guardian thought of being sacrificed. The guardian had protected Charthosk for the last five years and would now be thrown into a cauldron. Was the guardian ready?

Hans heard Felix on the platform, readying the crowd to throw Jasmine in. He heard no shame in Felix's voice. He did not hear a single noise of disapproval from the crowd. They were ready to see his friend burned away from existence.

Hans couldn't watch. He didn't want to look down at whatever Felix was getting ready to do. He stared solemnly at the tree top. Motionlessly. Desperately. Pleadingly begging for some miracle to happen.

Suddenly, he saw a flash of fierce green light from the treetop, a penetrating light that could've only come from the eyes of a human from Earth. No one else seemed to notice it.

Hans thought he was hallucinating. He blinked several times to make sure he was still sane. To make sure the events of the day hadn't driven him completely off the edge. The green light immediately faded away.

His breath became quicker. He could hear his heartbeat's intensity. The ominous green light terrified Hans almost as much as the sacrifice itself. Was the guardian somehow listening to his pleas?

The sun had almost set. The preparations were ready. Jasmine was lifted. Hans' knees could barely keep his weight up. He was seconds from crumbling down to the ground. His body would deteriorate and blow away in the wind.

Hans wanted to cry, but his eyes were as dry as that chip he had eaten.

He wanted to scream, but it felt like his vocal cords had been cut with a samurai's precision.

He wanted to exist, but every fiber of his body told him that death would be a salvation. That it would be easier for the train of time to take him away.

A branch bent out of form and started moving towards Jasmine. The entire crowd unanimously shifted their attention towards the branch. Other branches followed from various sides of the Mammoth Oak. The limbs of the tree were dancing and twirling through the air. There was a rhythm to their movement — an unheard tempo.

As Jasmine was thrown into the air, the branches caught her. Felix was taken aback. The people in the crowd began to stir. The absolute silence became a cacophony of voices.

It was the guardian. It had to have been. Was this the act of those green eyes that Hans had seen?

The branches moved in almost perfect form. To control so many branches at once, Hans guessed the perpetrator was a powerful Nature magician. It couldn't have been Jasmine. She was still unconscious in the air, gently emitting her flowery scent.

And she couldn't have cast any magic — her mouth was sealed tight.

In the perfect movement of the branches, there seemed to be a mistake Hans couldn't understand the motive behind. Jasmine's mouth was no longer sealed. The branches had cut the adhesive.

Jasmine noticed that she was no longer prevented from casting magic. She opened her eyes, awaking from the light slumber that Hans had thought to be unconsciousness. The smell she had been making began to lighten up.

Felix didn't seem to notice that Jasmine was awake as he talked with some of the ceremony's higher-ups behind the platform. Hans imagined they were desperately trying to find a way to remedy the situation. Felix mustn't have expected his luck to dry up.

Unfortunately for him, someone didn't want Jasmine to die so soon.

As Jasmine scanned the crowd, she stopped and looked carefully in a certain direction, which happened to be right at

Hans.

"Has she somehow recognized me?" Hans thought, observing Jasmine to see how she would react. A smile appeared on her face. As soon as she saw him, the smell disappeared. Hans wondered, *"Had that been for me to recognize her? Did she know I would be here?"*

Jasmine was satisfied with what she found in the crowd. She chanted, *"Atirgul trn raizginys. Ari roj."* Rosebuds started sprouting up from all around the Mammoth Oak. They completed their entire life cycle and achieved a perfect bloom in seconds. Jasmine was saving herself in style.

The roses clamped down with their thorns on the ropes and branches that were wrapped around Jasmine, stabilizing her.

But she wasn't done pulling tricks out of her sleeve. She had cast two spells at once. Jasmine was putting it all into these two spells—Hans wasn't sure she would be able to cast anymore.

As the roses created a little thicket of

hostile stems and regal crowns of red, pink, and white around Jasmine, aris started flying in from all different directions. The aris resembled bees. As one zoomed past Hans' ear, he caught sight of the familiar blue coloration of its fur.

Hans figured Jasmine's plan was to use the thorniness of the rose stems and the aris' stingers to cut down her restraints. The aris were noble in their sacrifice. Hans was certain she knew that bees on Earth die without their stinger. Aris were probably no different. But, at this moment, she was their queen. She had no honey to offer. And she couldn't be the aris colonies' salvation. But they were absolutely loyal. Just as the kiyik and the rodent had been to Hans.

The aris came in massive swarms. They started to pile up on top of each other, different colonies from all over Charthosk working together to appease their collective monarch. The aris shoved their stingers into the weakest parts of the ropes and branches.

Branches began to fall into the

cauldron. Ends of the ropes became frayed, unraveling and freeing Jasmine from capture. The roses moved her to safety.

The aris together created a moving symphony of buzzes. Thousands upon thousands of little bee-like creatures spun in the air, completing their given task and wearily flying back to wherever they came from, upset they would die for a false queen.

Many people in the crowd began to panic, backing away and running from the cauldron. The central marketplace was suddenly filled with an influx of traffic, which it struggled to handle. Movement was slow. The festival was not going as planned.

Felix finally noticed what was going on. He broke from his conversation to see Jasmine standing unbound on the platform, her ropes and the guardian's branches long inside the sacrificial cauldron. Her operation had been so fast and seamless that within a minute of chanting her spells, she had escaped.

Jasmine jumped down the stairs of

the platform. Her landing was unsteady. She stumbled, regained her sense of balance, and ran towards the crowd.

As she ran, Felix chanted, "*Shamol vortek*." His wings began to flap with increasing speed. Though a relatively weak two-word spell, Felix's raw magical ability made a powerful vortex appear above the cauldron.

The cauldron's boiling contents began to rise up. The fire under the cauldron was put out. The only light left to illuminate the Mammoth Oak against the evening-filled sky was the light coming from the marketplace.

Felix desperately tried to complete Jasmine's sacrifice. It would engrave him in history as the man to add an appetizer to the menu of the gods.

But Jasmine was smart in avoiding another capture. She had kept a small swarm of aris hovering around her. She used the aris to plummet through the remaining crowd towards Hans.

Her movement slowed. The vortex was desperately pulling her in. Most of her aris were yanked away into a concentrated space of high-speed winds and incredible turbulence. Hans made a mental bet that none of them would survive. That would be Jasmine's fate if he didn't act fast.

She extended her arm as her movement slowed to a halt. The vortex started to pull her back.

"Hans!" Jasmine yelled out.

Hans had been almost motionless since she was first presented on stage. Her escape had been a spectacle he couldn't understand.

But her yell broke Hans from his motionlessness. Here was his friend in front of him, asking to be saved. His crippling anxiety would have to wait its turn.

Hans reached back out to Jasmine, clasping her hand tight. He turned to run but realized he would be a victim of the vortex, too.

Hans glanced back at Felix. A wicked

grin found itself on Felix's face. He was satisfied, his wings flapping violently around him like a ravenous burgut who had spotted prey. He was confident it was over for Hans and Jasmine.

Hans was about to cast a spell. As he opened his mouth, he realized what would happen if he let words come out of his mouth. He was in the Crossroads, which was swarmed with people who had heard stories like the one told in the tavern. People who knew him only for the tales they'd heard of Celesmond.

"Do I really want to reveal myself here? Any magic, and they'd know the Terror had awoken." Hans was living his worst nightmare. Jasmine's face grew more distressed the more he waited in silence.

Hans looked again at Felix. His body was still, even though the vortex blowing right next to him was so fast that the wind was visible. Dust, leaves, and the contents of the cauldron were picked up increasingly rapidly, creating a tornado which sought carnage.

The wicked look on Felix's face reminded Hans of a woman that he had become acquainted with in the underworld of the Chaos Harbingers — Faye Jenegar. He had never considered Faye very beautiful, with her wicked appearance and the twisted way she looked at things. But she ran a well-oiled ship — the underworld of Vilemere.

Vilemere wasn't as innocent and flourishing as its government tried to portray. Faye headed an operation that stretched far beyond the city in influence.

Looking at the eerie way Felix stood, Hans was reminded of the true nature of Charthosk. He came to a decision. Sure, he felt shame being in Charthosk, and he would feel shame revealing himself as the Terror of the Forest. But he would not let himself die at the hands of this man.

Hans chanted, *"Barg kliziti."* He used the spell, knowing it would take a long time to arrive. He tried to hold his ground, clutching Jasmine's hand and fighting the terrifying pull of the vortex.

Leaves started to slither down the Mammoth Oak, reaching the ground like slender snakes. Some also started to slither in from the surrounding forest, slinking gracefully under the busy crowd.

As Hans lost his footing, the leaves stretched up in a chain, caught him, and pulled him back down to the ground. Nature spells were good in numbers and excellent when he was surrounded by a forest. The leaves set themselves down on his foot, acting like an anchor.

As he turned to run, his cloak tore off of his body. It had withstood the powerful winds for too long. With the cloak flew the heathers.

Alarmed, Hans yelped, "No!" mistakenly turning his head to look towards the cloak and heathers flying away. He made eye contact with Felix as the heathers got shredded in the high winds.

Felix's grin changed immediately to a face of horror. He had seen Hans' green eyes. It reminded Hans of his confrontation with Percival. Here was another man seeing the Terror of the Forest before him. Hans quickly turned back. He needed to take Jasmine and escape.

Felix wouldn't allow this. He immediately sprung to action to stop Hans. Hans couldn't hear what spell Felix used, but the vortex stopped spinning and concentrated itself into a wind column, just like the one Percival had expended all of his energy on only a few hours ago.

All the leaves that had anchored Hans from flying away into the vortex melded into a defensive formation, desperately trying to shield him from the incoming attack.

As Hans started to run, the attack shot out. The leaves were successful in robbing the attack of some of its energy, but it wasn't enough. Some of the wind pierced his shoulder, adding another injury to a growing list.

Hans staggered back. At least Jasmine had been ignored. More leaves slithered to his rescue, encasing him and Jasmine. This cocoon of foliage rose up, depositing them on the roof of the nearest food stall. It barely held their weight.

Hans looked back at the cauldron, which was now almost completely empty. Felix was talking to several other people in suits—security guards he had called to assist him in eliminating Hans and Jasmine.

Hans whispered, "Let's go." They were both deathly tired. But Jasmine simply nodded and followed.

They jumped from rooftop to rooftop in the direction of the Gentle Thicket. Hans figured they would be safe from their pursuers there. Tracking the two of them inside would be almost impossible.

Suddenly, Hans heard a flap of wings. Felix had given his orders and was now in the air, scouting for them. They were an easy find on the rooftops. They were also an easy target. Hans glanced at Felix. He looked like he was ready to destroy whatever it took to get rid of Hans.

But Felix was too late. Hans and Jasmine reached the edge of the Crossroads and jumped down from the roof of one of the stalls. Standing up was demanding because of their immense fatigue and brutal landing. But they dragged themselves up anyway. They could let the pain sink in later. Adrenaline ran them like a belligerent conductor.

Felix momentarily stopped flying, then began a barrel roll towards Hans and Jasmine. He was swooping in, ready to grab them. They slipped past the boundary of the Gentle Thicket.

Hans uttered, "*Ildiz blokada.*" Roots erupted from the ground and created a net at the entrance of the forest. They weren't as thick as the root Hans had used to protect himself from Percival. These roots were thin and surface-level, barely affecting the trees of the forest. But for the moment, it was enough.

Felix couldn't stop his barrel roll in time. He slammed into the net of roots, his arm just out of reach of either Hans or Jasmine. He clumsily stepped away from the net and attempted to enter through another opening.

People started to slip through the cracks between stalls, moving from the main streets of the Crossroads to the boundary of the Gentle Thicket. Both security guards and festivalgoers alike tried to see what had disrupted their peaceful evening so violently.

They couldn't go far past the alleyways of the Crossroads. Thin roots continued to shoot up at all entrances to the Gentle Thicket, blocking any chance of getting in.

Hans was a powerful magician. But the day had been long. He had two wounds — one that had long stopped hurting but was draining his abdominal strength and the newly opened one, which ignited terrible pangs of pain across his upper body. The roots took too much out of Hans. He collapsed to the ground. Jasmine collapsed to her knees.

As he lost the last of his energy, Hans could feel a root gently raise itself up beneath him. It began to wriggle deeper into the forest, moving him away from the harsh, bright light of the Crossroads. His vision became infested with silhouettes of trees and branches.

It was night in Charthosk. It was dark in the Gentle Thicket. And Hans was unconscious from fatigue, being carried away to an unknown destination.

CHAPTER 6

When Hans awoke, it was still night. He had only managed to get a couple hours of sleep. He propped himself up and looked around, trying to figure out where the root he summoned had taken him.

He was sitting in a treetop—a little nest created out of branches. He felt like a king as he looked down on the Gentle Thicket.

But Hans had no true dominion over the vast forest. Looking out from his vantage point, there were trees for miles. He was able to see the Mammoth Oak in the distance, looming over its tiny brethren.

What happened at the Crossroads

seemed like a distant dream. Or, at the very least, Hans wished it was.

He looked down at his body. He was surprised to see that his shirt was off. He was reminded of the scars he had accumulated from years of magical fights. The people of Charthosk could be ruthless.

Looking down at his lower abdomen, Hans remembered being incredibly well-built just a decade ago. His grandfather had ordered him to do tough training and he had obeyed. He had been like a beast. He realized now why people called him the Terror of the Forest.

However, Hans had lost it all. Years of inactivity made the fat return and the strength ebb away. Though he looked like a Viking in figure, he knew he wasn't anywhere near as strong as those legendary Scandinavians. He guessed he would be the lowest of the low in Earth Guild society.

Hans made a mental note to work out again. He didn't know if he would ever get a chance to or if he would ever again have the motivation.

His body wasn't only covered with fat and fading scars. There were bandages wrapped around the areas where he had recently been hurt—someone had treated his wounds. They had done it well, too, as he felt no pain moving around. He was still somewhat tired, but he knew that fatigue was the least of his issues.

As Hans wondered who had cared for him, his grandfather came to mind. *"Did he stay alive all of these years, hidden, just to heal me now?"* Hans asked himself.

The events of the previous day made a certain resentment well up for his grandfather. After all, he had been the one to rope Hans into all of it. He had been the one to plague Celesmond and leave the blame on Hans.

Hans wished he could talk with his grandfather and ask him why he did any of it. He wished he could punch his grandfather even though he knew it wouldn't make the pain go away. At the same time, he felt pitiful. The fear he had incited in Percival and Felix just by looking at them — was this his legacy?

Hans' thoughts were interrupted by a gentle hum behind him. He realized he hadn't looked entirely around since waking up on his timber throne. As he pivoted, he saw Jasmine, her eyes closed, on another tree. She was humming a pleasant melody. Hans let her finish.

"You weren't turning around, so I thought I would get your attention," Jasmine said after her last note, opening her eyes. She had on her usual overalls, splotched all over with paint stains.

Jasmine loved the views of Charthosk. She thought they were more beautiful than the ones on Earth. So she painted. It was her way of letting her mind escape, just like Hans with his little bonsai trees.

Jasmine wore her heart-shaped glasses. She had added little bee earrings to match her flowery fit. A rose stem slumped from a pocket in her overalls. Though it hadn't gotten sucked into the vortex, the petals were long gone. She didn't have on her usual cheery apron bearing the words "Jasmine's Flower Shop." Her clothes had slight rips and cuts around the cuffs of the arms and legs. There was a bruise on her cheek below her right eye.

Hans became angry at the people who had brought Jasmine to Charthosk. He figured she had been brought by force just like him. He couldn't figure out why.

There was an awkward moment of silence.

"What are you doing here?" asked Hans.

"Not even going to say hello, huh?"

"Sorry. Hello. What are you doing here, Jasmine?" Hans repeated.

"Oh, you never change, Hans," Jasmine laughed. "I'm not here of my own volition, as you might've guessed. I was dragged from my home a few days ago. Three men in black suits arrived at my little flower shop and pulled my unconscious body back into Charthosk. What a pitiful way to return here," she said, lowering her head into her arms.

"Percival, Lucan, and Emrys?" Hans asked.

"So you're acquainted with them too?"

"Yeah. Just like you, they came to my stationmaster's cabin and pulled me out. They were fast, I'll give them that." Hans paused. "What did they want with you?"

Jasmine raised her head to look at Hans. "They asked me where you were. I told them, 'He was a few blocks down from my shop, at the train platform. You barely missed him.'" A playful smile appeared on her face.

Hans was taken aback by this information. He hadn't expected Jasmine to sell him out like she did. He stared at her face for a couple of seconds, making sure this was still the same Jasmine he knew, who had worked alongside him in the MCIA.

Jasmine looked the same. But she

had let him be brought back to Charthosk, knowing that it could break him. She had seen his condition firsthand. In fact, Hans bet she was the only one who had witnessed his pathetic state after returning to Brumont.

"Why?" Hans demanded.

"Why?" Jasmine repeated. "Because you know how boring of a life you live. I wanted to get you up, traveling around Charthosk, reliving your youth," she said, looking into his face to see his reaction. Hans' face remained stone-cold—he was not easily amused. Especially not when it came to his experiences in Charthosk.

"I'm sorry," Jasmine continued when she saw that Hans wasn't interested in her playfulness. "They didn't beat me or abuse me much. Nothing like that. But I was stuck all alone. They told me that they would sacrifice me into that awful cauldron." She paused. It still wasn't enough for Hans.

She finally conceded, "You were the only person that could save me from that mess. I thought I could bring you to

Charthosk, and you would eventually find me. They said you had some heathers, so I told them they could've just asked me for a bouquet of them." Jasmine chuckled.

A small smile peeked out on Hans' face. It always amused him how Jasmine could find a way to be goofy, even in dangerous situations like the one she had been in, trapped by Felix and his goons. He didn't understand how she always got away with it.

She continued, "I think they were only interested in you, so they left me alone. I was stuck there, imagining how you would save me. And then you went and did it. I'll have to admit, those branches were impressive, even for you," Jasmine teased, glancing at Hans with a grin. He rolled his eyes. ". And then I raise my head and see this cloaked man amidst a sea of color, and I sense your presence, and I feel so free."

"Wait," Hans interrupted. "Branches?"

"Yeah. You know, the ones that came

down and stopped me from falling in. That was a nice last-minute save. I was so thankful. I honestly thought it was all over."

Hans thought back to the green gaze that had pierced through the Mammoth Oak's treetop. He remembered feeling crushed by that terrifying glare, helpless against a being more powerful than him. He wasn't sure who was behind the guardian's mask.

But the branches *had* come down and saved Jasmine. Both of them had witnessed it--a force of nature. A force of mercy.

"No. That wasn't me," Hans stated briefly. Jasmine looked at him quizzically. "I don't know anyone else who was there who would be able to use Nature magic. I don't understand who could possibly have done it."

Jasmine sat silently in thought.

"There *is* one idea I had. Right before they threw you in," Hans added, Jasmine wincing at his words, "I looked up at the grand tree. You know how the guardian lives up there, right?" Jasmine nodded. She imagined where this could be going but curiously listened in anyway. "I saw green eyes light up. I don't know where they were looking. I don't know to whom they belonged." Hans paused. "But I believe the guardian had decided to save you."

"Green eyes, huh? You know what that means."

"Yeah, but I don't know any other person from Earth that would be here after the MCIA collapsed."

They both looked down.

Hans asked, "Do you think it was him?" hoping that Jasmine would give him an answer she didn't actually believe in.

But Hans could hear the certainty in her voice when she responded with, "Yes."

Hans looked up at the sky above him. He had not taken a moment before to appreciate its beauty. The sky of Charthosk resembled Earth's sky. He believed that they existed at the same time but not in the same space. He was not sure of the true relationship between Earth and Charthosk.

All Hans knew was that his grandfather had stumbled upon this world and now seemingly made it his own. Had this man who wanted Charthosk to suffer snuck into the highest position and continued to terrorize its people? Hans did not understand his grandfather's motives. Hans was concerned about what had happened in the ten years that he'd been gone.

The sky was stunning. Away from all the pollution of Earth, everything was clearly visible. Unobscured by the light of distant cities, Hans could see the stars and constellations of the universe clearly. Any way his head turned, he was met with the void of emptiness that was space.

While the crescent moon found itself firmly in one position — unnoticeably moving around Charthosk, mysteriously illuminated by the Sun, which was fast asleep — the rest of the sky was populated by little dots of light. Humans had long formed patterns with these dots, creating connect-the-dots games for children to play, painting a rather boring canvas with a stroke of the careful organization that humans so adored, and giving names, stories, and meaning to wacky shapes and miserable polygons.

The sky was quiet. The stars just sat there, bodies of churning gases emanating light that took millennia to reach Hans' eye. The Moon was also quiet. Only a light breeze blew through the Gentle Thicket. Otherwise, it was silent. All the animals had stopped the cycle of life to have a rest.

Hans' mind was silent, too. He had so much to think about, but the day had taken too much out of him. He had just discovered that his grandfather was possibly the guardian. And he now sat in the middle of an unnavigable forest with his only friend. Hans took a deep breath. He wondered how he could get away from all of this.

Jasmine asked, "It's beautiful, isn't it?"

"What is?"

"This place, Hans." He noticed her also gazing up at the stars. "Charthosk."

"I know," Hans said, trying to signal he wasn't up for small talk at the moment.

"We were running past the marketplace while we were on the roofs. I took a second to look down, and I saw how active it was. I'm sure you noticed it, too, walking around earlier. This ceremony unites Chathosk. I know we've seen our fair share of disgusting things in this world, but all three factions have a lot of people who don't care about any political nonsense. It's sad that we had to get involved in all of it again," Jasmine said dejectedly.

"Do you know what I heard when I was walking around the Crossroads, Jasmine?" Hans asked.

"What'd you hear?"

"I heard stories about the Terror of the Forest."

"That's what they call you, right?" Jasmine laughed.

"Yes. The name may amuse you.

But they talked about the things I did at Celesmond. I've got to be honest, the storyteller was very good at his job. But I was upset that that's what they think of me now," Hans said.

"What you did at Celesmond? Come on, Hans, you can't seriously still blame yourself for that," Jasmine replied. "Your grandfather was the one who brought down his wrath on Celesmond. You were the face he used for the MCIA so he could get away with things. You can't be telling me you feel guilty for that. Grow up, Hans."

"Grow up?" Hans exclaimed. "Are you serious?"

"Yeah. Do you think I didn't feel awful after Celesmond? Fynn and Hayla were just the same. All of us were. Why do you think I've been painting so much? Your grandfather affected so many people beyond you, Hans." Jasmine's voice was rising in volume and aggravation. "But at least I'm not pitifully sitting in my house and trimming the same stupid tree over and over. Hans, what would you have done if I hadn't come to your house that day and told you to get a job? There has to be a limit."

Hans looked away. He was hit by words he didn't expect from Jasmine. He was hit by words he didn't want to hear. Here was someone telling him that the way he'd been living was wrong.

Hans had hidden from the world for ten years because he thought he no longer belonged in it. At times, he felt that it was wrong to waste away the rest of his life encased in absolute nothingness. In absolute complacency. But he continued on with his habits. He continued wallowing in shame.

"I'm sorry," Jasmine said softly.

"No, you're right," Hans responded. After a pause, he continued, "When I first came back here, I had a fight with the people who had captured me. You know, Percival, Lucan, and Emrys. I'm almost certain no one told them who they would be facing."

"Did you win the fight?" Jasmine interrupted.

"Yes, I won it, Jasmine. They weren't prepared at all. They said the guardian sent them to reclaim the heathers."

"Ah, the heathers."

Hans thought back to those heathers and how they had been destroyed. He wasn't sure if the ceremony actually ever needed the heathers in the first place.

"Afterwards, they called me treasonous, and we had our fight..." Hans trailed off, struggling to finish his sentence. "And then I had this crippling feeling. Like my mind was being consumed with all these different emotions from being back here."

Jasmine looked at Hans. She had a solemn look on her face, surprising to Hans amid her usual optimistic demeanor.

She said, "I think you're justified in feeling like you don't belong here. I just don't understand why you continue to feel like that on Earth. Your routine is based entirely on your crippling thoughts. And you've made no effort to change it. I understand your feelings. I know what happened feels more personal to you than to me. But please, Hans, the end of the world hasn't come."

"Yet," Hans joked in a rare show of humor. Jasmine regained her smile. "Well, I'll certainly think about it, Jasmine. I think this whole experience has required me to rethink something."

"I guess that's a start."

"But we have to figure out how to get out of here first," Hans pointed out. "Can't do anything trapped in Charthosk. What confuses me most is the heathers."

"What about them?" Jasmine asked.

"It's just... those heathers were handed to me by my grandfather a couple of years ago as a gift. They were standing in my cabin at the train station for the longest time. And yet the three men came and immediately went looking for them."

"And so the mystery intensifies."

Hans thought for a second. "So you think my grandfather's the guardian, huh?"

"Who else could it be? Nature user that has been in Charthosk for a long time and craves power. He checks all the boxes."

"I'm just thinking…" Hans said. "He gave me those heathers, and then he went and sent Percival and his gang to get them back. They said the heathers were sacred to Charthosk, that they're grown in the guardian's private garden, et cetera, et cetera."

"Really? I'd never heard of them being used in the ceremony before," Jasmine noted.

"Exactly."

Jasmine took a deep breath. She realized what they had to do to escape home. She explained, "We need to go back today, Hans. Perhaps your grandfather wants to see. If what we've guessed is right and he ends up being the guardian, today is his last day. The ceremony is going to happen, and we need to be there. It's our only chance."

Hans nodded but did not respond. He lay down for a second, giving himself the rest his body so craved.

Going back to the Crossroads would

be a death sentence. Felix had probably increased security after the incident just a few hours ago. They wouldn't want anything interrupting the sacred ritual of the guardian's sacrifice.

Hans wondered if he could just become a part of the Gentle Thicket. He could start his life anew as a hunter-gatherer—a simple life like the one he'd gotten used to.

But he understood that going back was his only option. He needed to meet the guardian. After all, his grandfather was the only person he knew who could transport people between Earth and Charthosk. If he could send them home, it would all be over.

Hans and Jasmine got up from their thrones in the treetops and jumped down, tumbling on branches and leaves until they reached the ground.

"I was awake while the roots were carting us away. While you were getting your beauty sleep," Jasmine said, looking at Hans mockingly, "I kept track, and I believe..." She pivoted around, searching for a direction. She chose a direction and pointed towards it. "We go there."

Hans didn't completely trust Jasmine. But he followed her anyway, his slight limp limiting his speed. He barely saw what was in front of him in the Gentle Thicket, since only some gentle moonlight illuminated their path.

He knew that none of it would be simple. But he was given an opportunity. At the very least, he had to try.

Hans and Jasmine planned as they walked. They decided they would hide out on the roof of a building and watch the ritual as it happened. They left this early in the morning so they could scout a location where they could see but not be seen before everyone was up and the ceremony was on its way.

They did not yet know how to get in contact with the guardian. They had no way to plan a meeting with him when they considered the gravity of the event they planned to attend.

The direction Jasmine chose turned out to be correct. Hans figured she used her Nature magic to create some map of the Gentle Thicket. Or she just guessed. With Jasmine, it was impossible to tell. Each step drew them closer to a bright source of light. This deep in the forest, it was inevitably the Crossroads.

As they approached the town, Hans saw the web of roots he had put up the night before. It stretched around a big portion of the outside of the forest in three layers. He was impressed with himself. He gently moved one of the roots aside and slipped through the crack, Jasmine closely following him. Keeping the barrier up would hopefully make it seem like they weren't up to anything.

They were now on the outskirts of the Crossroads and had to find a way to its center. They bravely walked through the main road of the town. The lights had been turned off to let people sleep.

Hans wondered where all of the

tourists rested at night. He noticed some stalls had housing firmly placed above them. He was sure the Crossroads stretched much further in the direction they were going, past the Mammoth Oak. There was probably a residential area there — hotels for the festive.

Other than a few straggler shops lit up to give sleepless men a nightlife, which Hans and Jasmine tried their best to avoid, the Crossroads was asleep. Hans realized how far the calmness of the night stretched.

Hans and Jasmine walked to the center of the Crossroads. Hans chanted, *"Barg kliziti."* Leaves yet again slinked out of the forest, lifting him and Jasmine up to the roof of a stall relatively close to the Mammoth Oak. The leaves shortly disappeared.

Now, Hans and Jasmine waited. They lay down flat in the middle of the roof they were on to make sure no one could see them until the morning. They didn't dare talk. Everybody at the Crossroads was probably aware that wanted criminals were present among them. They had to be careful as they sought a way to escape Charthosk.

Hans closed his eyes, allowing himself to doze off. The Crossroads was asleep, so he went to sleep, too. He had to get himself ready for whatever the morning had to offer.

CHAPTER 7

Hans was awoken by noise — people talking, utensils clinging, pots simmering, children laughing with firecrackers in their hands. It was the day of the ceremony. It was the day of the sacrifice.

He peeked over the edge of the roof. He understood why there was so much noise. The Crossroads was even busier than it had been the day before. Hans was astounded by how many people were moving around, congesting the poor town with suffocating traffic.

The area around the cauldron, which had its contents renewed after the vortex's rampage, was especially busy. Many people in suits were bustling about, peeking out of the colorful crowd, scouting for any disruptions to this sacred day.

For a moment, Hans felt safe. He was only peeking over the edge. People were so distracted by what was going on below that he doubted anyone would pay attention to him.

"Is it interesting?" Jasmine asked, still lying in the center of the roof. She had been awake when he fell asleep, and she was awake when he awakened. He was unsure if she had gotten any rest at all in the past day. She seemed to be shaken heavily by her kidnapping.

"Certainly," Hans responded.

"I'm glad."

Hans thought about what Jasmine had told him. She, too, was suffering because she had forcefully been brought back to a land she thought she had long put behind her. He respected her for keeping up her optimistic demeanor. At the very least, she didn't let other people know how much it affected her.

But Hans saw now that she, too, was a person with emotions. She was probably suffering the same crippling feelings he had felt earlier.

He didn't know if he would ever fully learn to trust himself again. But, for the sake of Jasmine, he needed to do something more with his life than building an army of beautiful shrubs. Maybe not in Charthosk. But certainly on Earth.

Hans' attention was caught by a particular group of suited gentlemen. Three in count, he noted. It was an Earth Guilder, a Sky Crusader, and a Chaos Harbinger. The Guilder was extremely well built, the Sky Crusader had massive wings trailing behind him—even bigger than the ones Felix had—and the Harbinger had a very long, slim tail and large horns.

Hans almost didn't recognize Percival, Lucan, and Emrys. They each possessed the qualities of the most respected members of their respective factions.

But a look at the men's faces confirmed that it was them. Hans tried to explain the situation to himself. They had probably used a disguising spell when they traveled to Earth. When he first fought them, it hadn't completely worn off. Now, they were conscious again, seeking revenge. He understood why they were *the* secret agents of Charthosk—they were terrifying in the canvas of mediocrity that made up the people at the Crossroads.

A realization hit Hans. He had worked as a secret agent to Charthosk under his grandfather in the MCIA. Percival, Lucan, and Emrys now worked under the guardian, who Hans was confident was his grandfather, as the secret agents to Earth.

Hans had been very loyal. And from their conversation the day before, these men seemed to be loyal, too. Hans' grandfather was good at getting people's trust. A terrible man with that level of influence scared Hans. "Why *was I so loyal?*" he wondered.

The men walked towards Felix, who

stood on the platform behind the cauldron. They engaged him in a deep conversation, all of them probably discussing Hans and the safety of the ceremony. Hans remembered the face of fear that had appeared on both Percival and Felix's faces when they saw his eyes flare green.

Suddenly, all four men started looking around. Hans felt an impulse to move back. As he started to crawl backwards, Felix made eye contact with Hans.

The last thing Hans saw before he crept back far enough was a creepy grin plastered on Felix's face—the same one he had when his vortex started dragging Hans and Jasmine into it, ready to tear them apart. It was over for Hans.

Hans stayed motionless for a second. He hoped that what he had seen was just an illusion. A hallucination. A dream. An imagined scene. Anything other than reality. He did not want to cast any spell. He did not want to tell Jasmine and worry her. He was as still as a statue.

Then, he heard the flap of two sets of wings.

"Jasmine!" Hans yelled. She shot up into a sitting position. But it was too late. Percival and Felix flew up into the air, almost immediately coming into Hans' view. In unison, they cast, "*Shamol neto.*"

Hans felt an enormous pressure drop on him. He couldn't see the net his captors had cast. The wind that wrapped around him was invisible but scarily dense. It sealed his mouth and shackled him tighter and tighter until he was trapped.

The net of wind started pulling Hans into the air. As Percival and Felix descended from their flight, the wind dragged him over the cauldron. He was powerless. He was going to be sacrificed. He was going to be the entrée before the main course.

"Ladies and gentlemen, we've got him," Felix proudly announced as he landed on the platform. He closed his wings and turned around, facing the crowd with a smile. "We present to you the Terror of the

Forest. Do not worry. We have constrained him. He has no chance of escaping." He paused, taking a moment to build suspense. Every silent millisecond felt like a mockery to Hans.

Felix continued, "You will now see an end to the legacy the Terror had left in Charthosk. He will die for his sins." A cheer erupted from the crowd. To Hans, it felt like a shot to the heart.

"Stop." The words rang out from the top of the Mammoth Oak. They were confident and booming, powerful and commanding. The voice was his grandfather's. Hans and Jasmine had been correct.

The crowd heeded the guardian's wish. Everyone who had heard his words stopped talking. Even Felix partook in the silence.

Hans was still suspended in the air, wondering if his grandfather would save him like he had saved Jasmine. He was sure Jasmine was still on the rooftop, panicking about his sudden departure. What could she do?

A lonely branch extended from the Mammoth Oak. It wasn't anything like the web of branches that had saved Jasmine. It was thick and sharp to a point. Hans was concerned. He didn't feel like he was being saved.

Hans' thoughts were correct. The branch shot right at his chest. He had a second to think. In that second, terror seeped through his mind. Through his fingers. Through his toes. He was going to meet a brutal end.

The second passed. Pain flooded Hans' body. His mouth filled with the taste of blood. He could no longer think. He could no longer breathe. A thick branch was stuck cleanly through his chest. Another second passed. Pain took up every bit of Hans' vessel of existence.

The crowd did not cheer. There was stunned silence. They had expected a sacrifice, not a murder. The branch started pulling into the tree, right into the guardian's den. It didn't matter anymore—Hans had blacked out.

CHAPTER 8

Hans did not understand how he was able to regain consciousness. He felt himself lying in a bed, seemingly alive. He stayed completely still, terrified that if he moved, he might discover that he had long been dead.

Slowly, he raised both his hands and clasped them. *"Real,"* he noted. He released his hands and touched the bed he was lying on. *"Real too,"* he told himself, surprised. Hans did not remember anything after the branch had pierced his chest. It was all supposed to be over after he blacked out. He was no longer terrified—he was dumbfounded.

As he thought about the branch, he looked down at his chest. Though there was a massive scar on its right, it looked like it had been repaired. Hans' thoughts of the afterlife returned. How was it possible for it to heal this fast?

He tried to prop himself up in his bed so he could look around, but pain forced him back down.

"I wouldn't recommend that," his grandfather's voice said to his left. Hans looked in the direction of the voice.

His grandfather wore the guardian's uniform, but the mask had been taken off. He sat in a chair at a wooden desk.

Hans and his grandfather were in an open space at the top of the Mammoth Oak, around which branches formed a cocoon, sealing the space off from the world. It was very minimalistic—filled with only a writing table, a chair, the bed Hans lay on, a kitchen, a small couch, and some pictures hanging on the side of a packed bookshelf. Hans swore one of the pictures was of him.

Looking at his grandfather, Hans noticed the age present on his face. There were wrinkles everywhere. It looked like he was trying to smile, but the smile didn't reach his eyes. He was supposed to die today in the ceremony. This was the face of someone who had lived too long for their own good.

"Well, Hans, it's been some time. I apologize for... that," Hans' grandfather said, waving at Hans' chest.

"Apologize? You almost killed me," Hans cried out.

"Well, what other way could've I used to get you up here? They were going to burn you. I pretended to kill you, then fixed you right up."

"Fix me up? There's this massive scar on my chest now," said Hans.

"Well, it adds to the collection," his grandfather laughed.

Hans didn't understand how he could be so nonchalant after not seeing his grandson for so many years, after what he did in Celesmond, after he shot a branch through Hans' chest. Thankfully, he had missed the heart.

Hans' grandfather dropped his fake smile. He looked at Hans and said, "Give the pain a few hours. My healing magic can heal some pretty bad stuff, but I guess since this pierced your right lung, it'll take a little longer to settle in." Hans understood now why his breathing wasn't as even as he had been used to his whole life. "Look, they're going to sacrifice me today. I wanted to talk to you one last time before I go."

"Why now?"

"Well, remember I gave you those heathers?" Hans nodded. "I was going to bring you back eventually with Percival and his guys. But... I don't know why I did it now."

"Hey," Hans said. He was staring at his grandfather, his eyes pleading for answers. He asked, "Why'd you do it?"

"You want the truth, don't you?"

"I do. About Celesmond."

"Why I did it, huh?" His grandfather explained, "Well, I was the first person from Earth to find Charthosk. When I was younger, I discovered magic. I spent a lot of time in Charthosk, exploring and whatnot. I'm sure you've seen how beautiful it is, right? We've gone on quite the adventures together."

"I guess that's one thing I can't deny about Charthosk—it's beautiful," Hans replied.

"Right. So, I tried to find people to explore this place with me. I ended up starting the MCIA. Although, at that point, it was just the MIA. The Magic Investigation Administration. Nothing with containment or whatever."

"Then what?" Hans asked.

"First, it was your father. He was my kid, and I was so proud of him. I tried to teach him magic when he was ready to leave home for college, but it ended up backfiring. His body just wouldn't accept the flow of magical power, even when I took him to

Charthosk. He eventually recovered, thank God, but he started to despise me. He hasn't talked to me since."

"I haven't talked to him much either. He left Mom when I was little," Hans said.

"I know. It was devastating to hear how much my son had cut himself off. I hope he's okay, at least." Hans' grandfather took a deep breath. "That was my first sour encounter with magic. I was very much obsessed with the academia of the Harbingers. They had so much interesting information about this world to teach. But when I was in Vilemere, I also saw the ugliness of the people here. There was this one woman who ran a whole underground operation to get revenge against her sister, who was the guardian at the time. She succeeded, creating a massive uproar throughout Charthosk. "

"Faye Jenegar?" Hans guessed, surprised at the new information he learned about her. He had been acquainted with her but had never heard of her murdering a guardian. His grandfather thought for a second.

"Yes, that was her name. I tried to keep you away from all of that. Never let you go to any of these festivals," Hans' grandfather said, gesturing down to the Crossroads. "Charthosk can be awful just as much as beautiful. The experiments they were doing in Vilemere with magic, under the moniker of innovation, disgusted me. And so, the MCIA was born."

"And then you brought *me* into it," Hans said.

"Well, your father was gone, your mother was struggling to take care of you, and you were little. Magic was like a daycare for you. I tried teaching you too, and it worked!" his grandfather exclaimed, his face lighting up with pride. "No wonder you developed to be very loyal to the administration."

"Celesmond," Hans reminded.

His grandfather's face grew grim. "Celesmond," he said, "was the first city with two factions living together. The Crusaders and Guilders had decided to improve their relationship and trade. Even one of the branches of Faye's operation found a home in Celesmond. I had seen too much of Charthosk at that point. Too much ugly stuff. I- I couldn't let them work together like that. So I destroyed it."

Hans' body shot up despite the pain. "That's it? Do you know what kind of pain I went through because of you?"

"I do."

"They all blamed me because you always used me as the image of the administration. While you hid in the shadows like a coward, they all saw me as the Terror of the Forest. The stories I heard in the tavern yesterday were awful. Do you think I want to be remembered falsely as a terrorist?" Hans shouted with increasing aggression at his grandfather. "Did you even *think* before you destroyed Celesmond?"

Hans' grandfather was silent.

"Answer me!" Hans continued.

"You're a coward! You took my loyalty to you — the fact I listened to your every word because I trusted you — and you went and made me suffer."

Hans couldn't maintain his position anymore. He winced severely because of the pain in his chest and fell back down onto his bed. He only noticed now his grandfather had also healed the other wounds he had received. His abdomen and shoulder were perfectly fine. Was this his attempt at repenting?

"I'm sorry, Hans," Hans' grandfather said.

"That's it, huh? That's all you have to say?"

"I'm sorry. I don't have any way to make it up to you. I tried to make it up to Charthosk. I went and used my healing powers for the good of the people. My unique skill meant I was chosen as the guardian. And I will ultimately pay the price for my sins by being sacrificed today. I have already accepted my fate."

Hans stared blankly at the ceiling of branches and leaves of his grandfather's treetop abode. He had not expected what his grandfather told him. He thought his grandfather had become the guardian as another power grab. Hans was surprised he had shown remorse.

The train of time had hit Hans' grandfather with reality. All of his blunders had come tumbling down as the MCIA collapsed, as Hans' life collapsed. He hoped his grandfather felt severe guilt after what he did to Celesmond. The fact he would be sacrificed made Hans feel like he had found a way to pay the world back—with his death.

Hans' grandfather continued, "I brought you here because I wanted to say goodbye one last time. Thank you, Hans, for trusting me. Even if it doesn't seem like it anymore, it meant a lot," he said solemnly, pausing for a moment to listen. "It's almost my time. Listen to the people below."

During the conversation, Hans had

heard distant cheering and singing. The crowd probably thought that the Terror of the Forest was slain by their mighty guardian. A joyful mood emanated through the people who were waiting for the ceremony's end. To them, their guardian had performed his final task. The people of Charthosk, at least, had found closure.

"I was the first human here. I am the one capable of transporting people. I brought you here. And when I die, you will be forced out, back to Earth. Hopefully, ties between the worlds are severed. If they're not, never come back here," Hans' grandfather said. "You do not belong in Charthosk. I realize now none of us ever did. But when you get home, please don't let yourself be bogged down by what I did. They were my crimes. And I paid for them. The people of Charthosk think you're dead. I'm sorry your legacy was tarnished here. But please… live like it was untarnished when you're on Earth."

There was a knock on the door. Hans looked to the left of his grandfather. There was a staircase leading out of the tree, and at the bottom of it was a door. Nobody opened the door. But the knock was a good enough indication--it was time.

"Goodbye, Hans."

"Goodbye… grandpa."

Hans lay in bed and thought about what his grandfather had said. His thoughts flowed like a river. They gushed down the side of a cliff—falling perpetually, splitting into tiny water particles, and drizzling down into the ocean that was his mind.

Hans had experienced a lot in Charthosk. He had obeyed his grandfather until he came to his senses and realized he had followed too far. He felt like he had been a soldier, perfect and neat. He had been like one of his little bonsai trees, part of a small army of people who his grandfather had indoctrinated. But it wasn't as careful a process as Hans' weeks-long bonsai trimming. Parts of him had been chopped away until he was bare, empty, and pitiful.

But nature is complex. Nature heals.

Even awfully trimmed bonsai trees can grow into something that can be appreciated. Hans did not know how long it would take for his bonsai tree of existence to bloom. All he knew at the moment was that he wanted to watch the ceremony.

Hans dragged himself off of the bed. He noticed his pain had subsided. His grandfather's time in Charthosk had made him an effective healer.

Hans was able to stand long enough to walk to the edge of the cocoon of branches he was in. As he sank to the ground, peeking through the cracks in the branches, he saw his grandfather walk out, met with a cheer from the crowd. He had put the guardian's mask on. His features were completely hidden from the world.

Most citizens of Charthosk probably didn't know who their guardian really was. They did not know that he was the one who had terrorized Celesmond. That he was the one who had headed the invasive MCIA.

But, at this moment, none of that

mattered. They trusted him, and he had done his job. Now, it was his time to save the land from decay. He was their savior, whether his past should've allowed that or not.

Hans' grandfather stepped onto the platform, escorted by Felix, Percival, Lucan, and Emrys. As Felix made a speech, his grandfather stood motionless, probably readying himself for the final moments of his life.

Hans barely heard Felix's words. And he certainly couldn't tell what Percival, Lucan, and Emrys were telling his grandfather. He was sure they spoke sentimental words. After all, they had served under a persuasive leader who they now had to see go.

The speech was over. The cauldron was boiling hot. Felix called up onto the stage people to throw in the other ingredients necessary for the sacrifice. Hans made out a kiyik and various herbs and flowers. None of them heathers. It really had just been a way to get him into Charthosk again.

The preparations were over. Percival cast a spell that picked Hans' grandfather up into the air. The guardian was now above the cauldron. The people in the crowd collectively said a chant to bless Charthosk for another five years.

Hans' grandfather was dropped in. It was soundless. It was almost rippleless. He did not float back up to the top. The cauldron made quick work of his body, melting his existence away.

For the first time in a very long time, Hans cried. Tears streamed down his face. He had no love for his grandfather. He still did not completely forgive him—a sorry just didn't cut it. But his grandfather was respectable. The train of time had come to take him away, and he complied, wordlessly and nobly.

Hans' adventures with his grandfather were over. His adventures in Charthosk were over. He couldn't help *but* cry.

Suddenly, Hans felt a jolting feeling.

Charthosk was telling him he didn't belong. His grandfather was dead. The key had been taken out of the lock, and "*qulf blizu*" had been cast.

Hans imagined Jasmine was feeling the same thing. The feeling became crippling. He closed his eyes, trying to get rid of it. He didn't open them again for a long time.

CHAPTER 9

A train whooshed into the station, reeling as it braked to a stop. The doors opened, and the conductor announced that they would be taking a short break before departing for the next station.

The last time Hans was on a train, he had been riding it involuntarily. That train's next station had been one fraught with conflict and near-death encounters.

But as the conductor announced that the train would depart soon, Hans was finally ready to see the train's next destination willingly. Five years as a stationmaster and he had never once explored past Brumont. That was all about to change.

Hans looked to his left. Jasmine was standing next to him, even more excited than he was. They were going to explore wherever the train would take them together.

"It's nice seeing you out like this, Hans," Jasmine said, turning to him.

"I know." Hans took a deep breath. "I know."

After being teleported out of Charthosk, Hans had been plopped back on the Brumont train platform. Though his breathing had restabilized, his ribs still hurt from being pierced by his grandfather's branch. So he limped home as fast as he could. As soon as he reached his bed, he immediately collapsed asleep. Charthosk had been too much for this body.

Upon waking up, Hans learned just how powerful his grandfather's healing magic was. Though scars remained from his injuries, there was no pain. He was glad he had recovered so quickly.

Hans learned that nobody at Brumont ever realized he or Jasmine were gone.

Percival, Lucan, and Emrys had probably used some form of concealing magic to make everyone who had been at the train station unaware that Hans was being kidnapped, leaving them confused as to why the stationmaster was taking a vacation without a substitute.

Hans and Jasmine had also been in Charthosk for such a short period of time that nobody had become suspicious. At the very least, this allowed Hans to forget about what happened. He was home, confident he would never go back.

But he realized in the following days that there was no way to forget what happened at Charthosk. He tried to enjoy the monotony of life again. He continued with his stationmaster job, watching the trains come into the station on their constant schedule. And as soon as he came home, he trimmed bonsai trees to perfection. But Hans was thinking the whole time.

He thought while he sat in his little stationmaster cabin. He thought while he looked around at the trinkets he had on his shelves — his favorite bonsai tree, the yet-unopened candle from his mother, the massive timetable that had once told him train times, the space missing its pot of magical heathers. He thought while he trimmed bonsai trees, which severely cut down the efficiency he had built up over the years. He thought while he walked home and while he walked to work.

Two people had told Hans to consider exploring the world outside of his minimalistic life. And Hans now wanted to try it, too. He had seen the beauty of Charthosk--the scenery, the animals, and the festivity of Charthosk's factions. Earth was probably just as beautiful, too.

But Hans couldn't confirm Earth's beauty. It now saddened him that he didn't have any such stories or memories. He no longer felt fulfilled doing the same thing over and over. He yearned for something more.

His yearning brought him to Jasmine's

door. Hans hesitated before knocking, mentally calculating whether this was really what he wanted. He took a deep breath and tapped his knuckles three times on the birch door.

"Coming!" Jasmine called.

Hans waited a few minutes. Each minute increased his desire to run away. But he stayed in place—he had made himself a promise. Eventually, Jasmine opened the door. She had purple hair rollers in her hair and a pink bathrobe around her body. Her hair smelled slightly of honey. Jasmine looked Hans up and down.

"Well, Hans Eindride. I wasn't expecting to see you here. What brings you to my door?" Jasmine asked.

"So, I was thinking…" Hans trailed off.

"Uh-huh," Jasmine encouraged.

"I'd like you to come with me somewhere outside of Brumont."

"Wait. Hans. You did not just say that."

"I believe that I did," Hans said.

Jasmine ran up to Hans and hugged him. He hadn't expected a hug from her. He didn't get a chance to react before Jasmine ran back inside, shouting, "Give me just a few minutes."

As she entered her house, she slammed the door in Hans' face. He stared at the door, startled for a second. Then, a big grin appeared on his face. He breathed in the fresh Brumont air, filling every single cell in his body with oxygen. His breath out left him a deflated balloon. Hans made sure all the Charthoskian air was out of his system. This was his triumphant celebration.

Hans and Jasmine chose to go to a town near Brumont called Tuskenvale. The town wasn't any less dull than Brumont — there wasn't much interesting to do in the region Hans lived in. But it was a start. They would see what Tuskenvale was like. They had dared each other to find some way to enjoy Tuskenvale.

Then, another day in the future, they

would explore further places. More exciting places. Like the ones Percival, Lucan, and Emrys had hung up on their walls.

Hans now stood before the train that would take him on his journey outside of Brumont. To him, there was nothing out of the ordinary about this train. All he knew was that it would bring him safely to Tuskenvale. But assumptions are often dangerous. After all, the train of time now stood at its destination.

The train of time forever carries sins and blunders. Like predatory passengers, they sit in neat rows, awaiting the train of time's arrival at its next stop. They patiently bide their time, ready to remind the next passenger of all their vices.

But the train of time isn't evil. It is simply a vessel of a person's life. In its reign over that human, the train of time carries their dreams. Behind its perfect timetable, the train of time carries their memories. Memories of sins and blunders. But also memories of happiness and satisfaction.

Where the person decides to sit defines how they see their past.

When Hans stepped on the train before him, with Jasmine following close behind, he was a passenger to Tuskenvale, ready to explore an unknown location. What he was oblivious to was that he had boarded the train of time. But he did not sit in the packed cabins of sins and blunders. He did not sit in the cabins of warm and welcome memories. He walked firmly to the conductor's spot and took command of the powerful locomotive. After all, Hans was free.

THE END

Aleksey Olkhovenko was born in Uzbekistan and currently lives in New York City. He is an emerging fantasy author with a love for fictional worlds, which originates in his childhood love for reading. Aleksey's debut novella takes place in one of these worlds — a land called Charthosk — where former secret agent Hans gets kidnapped and where he must face his troubled past.

When not writing, Aleksey is a nationally-ranked public speaker for his school's speech and debate team and one belt away from becoming a black belt in Taekwondo. As a debut author, Aleksey is working on larger projects, including the completion of a full-length novel.

Though new to the craft, he writes every day to hone it, improving his prose and getting better at crafting stories with his unique voice.